The Corn Maze

By Kaye Giuliani

Text copyright @ 2014 Kaye M. Giuliani

All Rights Reserved

To my Aunt Pam, who encouraged me to keep telling outrageous stories.

Table of Contents

The Corn Maze 1
Water 11
Backtracking 16
Skink 22
Busy Hands 27
Cheyenne Name 34
Heat and Light 39
Ahqui's Quest 42
Shelter from the Rain 44
The Bad Place 47
The Gift of Fire 50
The Harvest 53
Mama Bear 59
The Rock 63
Sleepless in 67
"Where the Fuck am I?" 67
Terminal Rock 73
The Natalo Tribe 78
Carried Away 88
A Fugitive among Them 94
The Wise Man of Agrigar 101
The Closed Door 109
The First Attempt 113

First Confession	117
Rhamas is Wise	120
The Wedding	127
The Word of the Law	133
The Interrogation	136
Trippin'	144
The First Night	149
A New World	154
The Ghama Traya	159
Touching the Stone	165
Where the Fuck are We Now?	169
The Paclusin of Montaroon	176
The Hills Are Alive	183
Death at Dawn	188
The First Jurrah	194
The Inhabitants of Heaven	200
Reconnaissance	205
Heavenly Bodies	211
Return and Report	216
Memories of Love	227
Clearing the Air	232
Meeting Xiri	240
Xiri of Montaroon	247
The Cart with no Oxen	251
Developer's Nightmare	260
Going Home, at Last	263

High Rise Heaven 268
Dynamite 274
The Earthquake 276

The Corn Maze

Alisha dug into the pocket of her jeans for a fiver and handed it to Mrs. Weaver. The Weaver family owned the field that sponsored the corn maze every autumn, and often extended family members took turns handling admissions. In addition to the maze itself, they offered hay rides and pumpkin sales. At the peak of the season, there was even a snowball stand set up at the exit to snare thirsty explorers. The maze was one of Alisha's yearly traditions, so when Mrs. Weaver cautioned her not to "get lost in there," Alisha swept past her with a confident laugh and a dismissive backward wave.

She sighed deeply as the rows of corn closed around her. Alisha was grateful that there had been no lines. She hated being crushed between the giddy preteens and the meandering parents with their whining babies.

Alisha had a sixth sense for puzzles and mazes, so, today wasn't about the challenge it presented, but about the solitude that came from being curtained off by towering walls of silk-tasseled cornstalks. The sounds and smells took her to a simpler place. A country life: cows and horses – barns, and little pink piglets... and away from the rows of plastic,

Monopoly-game houses and matching concrete driveways that made up her day-to-day reality.

Alisha padded on, taking only right turns for a long way to get the lay of the maze. She drew in deep breaths of the crisp air and listened to the gentle swishes and crackles of the stalks. "Aha!" She thought to herself as she reached the first dead end. So, this wasn't the standard right-turn maze. Hmm. She could backtrack and try left turns for a while, or she could just wander about with no plan, whatsoever.

It was here that Alisha made her first mistake. She decided to wander through the maze without a plan. The day was cool, and it was still early. Why not stay in the maze for as long as possible? Five bucks wasn't anything to sneeze at, you know. Especially when all of the proceeds from your summer jobs had gone towards the purchase of your first, used, battered, badly-in-need-of-a-paint-job car.

"My own car." Alisha mooned, as she plodded happily through the corn, making rights and lefts wherever she pleased. School had already started. Her senior year. Those who had considered her a friend had been happy to see her, and the rest (the majority) had finally matured enough to no longer give a damn one way or the other. It was a new kind of freedom. For the first time, Alisha was happy to be herself, and didn't have to work so hard at invisibility. She had started to daydream about a future that would be bright with achievements and personal glory, and a car...

The 64 Pontiac Catalina turned in her imagination as though on a showroom pedestal. Glints of teal and chrome rotating slowly under bright lights. She wondered what the male population of Sentry Heights Sr. High would think as she pulled into the high school parking lot for the first time and coolly switched off the ignition of that car. Wow.

Of course, there were some minor repairs that needed to be made before it was actually "drive-able." It leaked oil and brake fluid (and just about everything else according to her brother, Skink). But, it was a historic car, after all, and she knew he would be happy to pull it all apart and put it back together again. That was kinda' what Skink did instead of sports. It was a "Man" thing, and it was what bought him passage to the "Manly-Man" brotherhood that bound all penis-bearing humanoids in a holy and exclusive alliance.

See, he was tall. Skink was like six foot seven. A giant, really. Everybody wondered why he hadn't gone out for sports, but she knew. Skink was a major clod. Like, he had the grace of a three-legged anteater. Besides which, Skink didn't care whether or not somebody snatched a ball out of his arms and ran away, sneering. He wasn't at all territorial. That sort of thing just didn't inspire him to battle. There were lots men like him, and they became car mechanics or professional skateboarders or parked their testosterone allotments in similarly acceptable slots, elsewhere.

Nope, "patient," "silent," "steady" were the words that described him best. He could fix anything, and often did. It gave him a certain popularity that Alisha had never known, and she envied him that.

Today was hers. While Saturdays were usually Dad's best opportunity to exert his authority and instruct his adoring household in the virtues of cleanliness and order, today had started out differently. Two post-it notes on the fridge had advised that Dad would be working downtown, there was sandwich meat in the fridge, and Mom (no fool, Mom) would be "running errands" and didn't expect to return until 6:00 or 7:00 that night. Alisha translated "running errands" to mean "shopping and lunching" with Gail and Linda – Mom's two partners in crime. She smiled. A glance into Skink's bedroom was all she needed to know that he would be power-sleeping until one of two things happened; he got hungry; or he had to pee. All, in all, it was a perfect day. Alisha's perfect day.

It was quite a while later, when she began to get hungry

and thirsty, that Alisha realized that she had no idea how to get out of the maze. She was lost. She turned in a complete circle and stood on her toes to peek over the stalks, but they were too high. She listened for the sounds of the Webber Junction traffic to get a sense of direction, but could hear nothing(?) Webber Junction was the only road through town and was seldom quiet. She reached for her cell to check the time.

"It couldn't hurt to check out the GPS, too." She laughed at herself. "A GPS to get out of a corn maze."

The phone wasn't there. Oh. Right. She hadn't thought she would need it, and, well, she didn't need it, really. If worse came to worse, she could always just follow one row of corn out to the end.

Alisha took in a deep breath and stretched. The air was much cooler now. She found herself wishing she had thought to bring a jacket or put on some shoes instead of her favorite flip flops. Her heart was troubled, but Alisha pushed worries aside, chose a direction, and moved half-sideways to follow a row out of the field without trampling the maze.

"How far could it be?" She chided herself. The maze only occupied the width and breadth of your average football field, and anywhere she came out would be only blocks from her home. She went on this way – crab walking – for long enough to have crossed four football fields before she turned and began to mash and crash her way forward. She was out of breath, and cold, and terror was beginning to take hold. Where was the end? She should be home by now, soaking her dirty feet in a hot tub and laughing at herself for being so foolish. The sun was going down, for chrissakes, and the only sounds she could hear were the swishing of the corn husks, and her thudding heart.

Something was very, very wrong. Alisha had read enough fantasy and sci-fi novels to know when she had stepped out of her world and into another. There were a lot of people to whom such a thought would never occur. Alisha, however, had always left room in her mind for doors to other dimensions, and was of the firm belief that this qualified her for entry.

"But, even in another reality the corn would come to an end." She laughed, nervously, rubbed her hands together, and noticed for the first time how they were latticed in tiny cuts and covered in a fine film of dust.

Finally, too exhausted to move on, she stomped out her own crop circle and decided to call it "home" for the night. Falling to a seated position almost hurt more than it helped.

The delicate flesh between her big toe and the next toe over (what did they call that toe?) was blistered and stung like the blazes. Her feet were filthy with the dust of the fields, and she suddenly became aware of the ache in her arms, back and thighs.

She huddled there with the night sky for a ceiling and wondered what her family was doing at home. Where did they think she had gone? Was anybody even worried yet?

Those questions brought her heartbeat back to a painful hammering and she swallowed nothing down a dry throat. Weren't there snakes in cornfields? And... rats?

Again, Alisha stilled her body to listen, but heard nothing. She hadn't heard anything other than herself for hours. The evening sky was free of clouds, and it wasn't long before she had a virtual ceiling made up of the moon and a million stars to gaze up at. But, not one bird. Not one bat. It was getting to be a toss-up as to which was creepier, the lack of living things, or the thought of them sneaking up on her for a nibble while she slept.

Eventually, Alisha did sleep and awoke to another perfect autumn morning. The sun had already been up for hours – she surmised – guessing it to be somewhere around

9:00 a.m. Things have a tendency to look better after a night's sleep and she stretched luxuriously before rising to brush cornfield from her clothes and hair. Wouldn't this be a great story someday?

"Remember that time Alisha got lost in the Weavers' corn maze and spent the night thinking she had wandered into an alternate universe?" Laughs all around.

She listened for the sounds of traffic that would lead her back to the road, and then home. Silence.

Okay. What now?

She needed a vantage point before deciding in which direction she was going to head, and cast her eyes about for a solution. Of course, there was only corn and more corn. Okay, she said with determination, then, corn it will be.

The stalks were thicker than Alisha had first imagined and her hands were bare. You could break them off if you bent them back and forth after stomping them into submission. Still, the pile grew too slowly and her hands were becoming raw and blistered. One look at the sun and Alisha could see that she was burning up too much of the day on this project. She was thirsty and her stomach was starting to burble with hunger. She flopped down upon the meager pile of cornstalks and wiped her face on the hem of her tee shirt.

She knew that the maze had always been planted with feed corn – the kind you scooped into buckets for the livestock. The kernels were often multicolored and hard as pebbles on the ears. So, it was without a great deal of optimism that she reached for an ear and pealed back its husks.

Alisha was puzzled to find that the corn in her hands was not feed corn, at all, but bright yellow, tender and sweet corn that was meant for people.

"I'm people!" She said aloud.

Though troubled anew by this discovery, she was too hungry to be disappointed. Alisha stripped the ears right down to their cobs, and didn't stop until she was full.

Hunger satisfied, Alisha returned to mound up the stalks until the pile had reached a height of two feet or more. She paused before stepping up, closed her eyes, took in a deep breath and formed positive thoughts.

"I will see the roads, the neighborhood, the entrance gate – and I will feel like an ass -- but be home before dinner."

With hands clenched, she stepped to the middle of the pile and listened to it compress and shrink under her weight. But, there... Yes! She could see above the corn at last! She saw... more corn.

With a tear of frustration forming in her eye, Alisha turned in a slow circle, scanning the horizon. Suddenly, way off in the distance, she could see a great dark forest. Her heart flipped oddly and brought with it a constricting pain. It was clear that, well, she wasn't in Kansas anymore. There was nothing but corn on three sides. No smoke from fairytale cottages or castles on hilltops or any of the things one would expect to encounter in an alternate universe.

Water

Alisha was too tired to cry and too stubborn to be truly afraid.

"Hey, look at me. I'm the heroine of my own fantasy novel." She croaked out loud to nobody. "Trees need water, and so do I, so... next stop – creepy-as-crap dark forest."

Alisha set off in that direction with hopes of reaching the woods before nightfall. Along the way, she had taken to pulling a kernel or two off passing ears of corn and sucking on them to relieve her aching thirst. The thought of water powered her forward long after her spirit of adventure had shriveled up and dropped from the vine. Still, she knew her destination, and she knew she would arrive there eventually – which was more than she had to go on the day before.

At last, the corn fell away to reveal a narrow band of dirt and weeds that lay between the field and the forest. Being able to go no further, she fell to her buttocks and collapsed to bury her face in the relative softness of the weed-cushioned dirt.

Water.

She knew she would have to find it soon or she would

die.

"I could *die* here." she thought, without alarm. "I could die right here where I'm sitting and nobody would ever find me or know what happened to me."

This thought appealed to Alisha's sense of drama. "My face will be all over the television and on milk cartons. My brother will cry on Oprah. Wow. I really hate to miss that."

She sat up and covered her face with both hands. "God, I hope Mom doesn't give them last year's school photo."

But, even as the thought formed, Alisha knew that her famous milk carton debut would have a dopey expression, an exposed bra strap and one eye half closed. She winced, inwardly.

Water.

Thirst commanded more forward motion and Alisha reluctantly complied. In moments, the dark canopy had closed over her head and her journey through the deep woods had begun. At first, the undergrowth had been thick and difficult to travel through, but, gradually, the trees grew larger and the canopy blocked out much of the sun that the brambles and ferns would have needed to thrive. This part was easier going.

Leaves of all colors dropped gently to the ground as she

made her way deeper into those enormous trees. She kept her eyes and ears alert for any sign of a creek or stream. As she walked, Alisha tried to remember how the survivalists found water on TV specials, but only came up with the thing about licking off morning dew from the leaves. She cast her eyes upward at the distant branches and gave up on any thoughts of climbing. Besides, morning was a long way off. Discouraged, but determined, Alisha continued to trudge forward.

Water?

She was thinking it must be early evening when the sound reached her ears. Water. It was running somewhere nearby. The sound was maddening, and she half-ran, half-stumbled towards it for what seemed an eternity before the trees parted once again to reveal a wide and briskly-flowing stream. Her first instinct was to bury her face in it and suck up as much water as she could hold, but, what had that guy said on TV about parasites? Shouldn't she boil it first? No. She couldn't boil it, but...

Alisha grabbed a rock with a jagged edge and started digging a hole near the edge of the stream. Before long, the hole had filled with muddy water and she dipped into that to drink and drink and drink. It was gritty, yes, but the survivalist had said that water filtered through sediment was less likely to contain contaminants, and therefore safer to drink. She was proud of herself for remembering that trick, and hoped that the guy wasn't just full of crap. She looked, longingly, at the clear cool rushing water and dipped up another handful of floating sediment.

She tugged off her flip flops and examined her feet. It wasn't good. Why couldn't she have worn a pair of sneakers with socks? Maybe tied a hoodie around her waist, or something? Unable to resist, she thrust her feet into the cool, rushing water and watched the dirt lift away and float downstream.

"Ahhhh." Flesh-eating bacteria be damned. That felt good.

Having had her fill of water, Alisha looked around. She saw only familiar trees, Oak, Maple, Sassafras, Mulberry, Ash; nothing at all alien or strange. There was, however, an alarming lack of birds, squirrels, and rabbits. Sitting there, she could believe herself to be the only living creature in the universe.

Pulling from 'The Wizard of Oz' again, she wondered "Where are the Lions, Tigers and Bears? Oh my!"

Bears? Jeez. She scanned the woods again for any signs of life. "C'mon." She said out loud with some disappointment, "No talking unicorns or magic goldfish? What kind of fantasy novel is this, anyway?" Her words dropped without consequence onto the forest floor like so many leaves.

On her hands and knees, she searched the shallows of the stream for any signs of life: minnows, or salamanders – even a dragonfly – but there was nothing. Alisha was really and truly alone.

As the evening wore on, she began to shiver in the chill. There was nothing for it but to curl up as tightly as possible and sleep, and that's what she did.

Backtracking

A stiff and half-frozen Alisha awoke to find a new day in what she was now affectionately referring to as "The Land of Where-the-Fuck-Am-I."

Alisha wasn't the type to punctuate sentences with four-letter-words. She had experimented with the concept in middle school, only to discover those words did not sound natural coming from her face. Alisha's face was plain, open, and (she liked to think) intelligent. She had the face of a 'nerd,' to put it in the vernacular of her time. Therefore, dropping "F" bombs only served to draw attention to the fact that she was trying too hard to fit in.

But, in the privacy of her own skull, where nobody was apt to be offended, she pulled from her entire vocabulary the words that seemed most appropriate to each situation, and, clearly there were times when the "F" bomb was the correct choice. This being one.

Once again, Alisha was faced with some hard decisions. She made a mental list of all the good advice she had gathered over her limited lifetime.

1. When you get lost – stay put until you are found.
2. Follow a river downstream to find areas of human habitation.
3. Use the moss on trees to ... um. (Was that North or South with the moss on it? Something to do with the movement of the sun... Oh, screw that one).
4. If your path grows more and more treacherous – backtrack.

Backtracking. She shivered. The very thought of venturing back into the sea of corn left her shaken. Still, that advice had made the most sense. Could she find her way back? Did she want to find her way back?

Now there's one question I'd never thought to ask.

"Of course I do!" Everything was said aloud at this point. Hearing her own voice was somehow comforting. "What kind of logic dictates that forging further ahead will take me back?" Heading for the forest had been the only thing to do before, because she had needed water so desperately. In building the mound of stalks, her goal had been to see her way to the main road in her world – how could she have known that there would be no main road? No neat rows of vinyl sided suburban siblings?

Up until this moment, she had made mostly logical choices. Right?

Alisha hung her head and hugged herself. "I should have stayed on the maze paths. This happened because I tried to escape the maze to save time. Why didn't I just stay on the paths?" That started her pacing compulsively, running fingers through her shoulder-length dark brown hair and removing pieces of crumbled leaf and twigs from the snarliest bits.

So, now she had a dilemma. Either find her way back through the cornfield, or forge ahead in the hopes of finding...what? Would there be humans in this reality? Surely, someone had planted all of that cursed mess of corn.

"Won't someone come to harvest it?" Her hopes lifted somewhat. If that was the case, all she had to do was make herself comfortable here until they showed up. Alisha was no agriculturalist, but that corn was ripe for the picking.

She assessed her surroundings more critically. "I've got water. I've got corn. The dried husks I've been walking on for days will make good kindling if I can find a way to generate a spark." Alisha winced, inwardly. She had watched three full seasons of "Survivor," and knew that sparks were hard to come by. There were plenty of saplings and fallen trees for building a makeshift shelter, however.

Or...

She could backtrack. That made the most sense. After all, she had no idea exactly *what* would show up to harvest the corn. Or, how much those whatever-they-weres would appreciate her presence... What if they found her, say, *delicious*? Alisha imagined being served up as "Long Pig" and dismissed the troubling image away with a wave. If she decided to re-trace her steps, then she would need to find a way to carry water along.

Alisha leaned against the nearest tree and pursed her lips in thought. What would a "Survivor" contestant do? In past episodes they had used hollowed gourds, man-made containers that had washed up on shore and animal bladders... She crossed her arms and sighed, rolling her eyes heavenwards for inspiration.

Nothing.

"Think!" she repeated with rising frustration.

It was at that moment Alisha heard a tiny sound to her right. She froze in place, just listening. There it was, another displaced twig, the infinitesimal shuffle of dried leaves. Without breathing, she turned her eyes towards the sounds. There was a thing looking up at her with no small amount of curiosity. She wondered if it had a bladder – but only for an instant – dismissing the thought as rude.

"Hello little thing." She ventured, half turning in slow motion. "Where did you come from?"

It stood up on two hind legs and sniffed the air. Alisha sought descriptive categories that might apply. "Bear," "squirrel," "timid," "inquisitive," "large-eyed," "opposing thumbs?" Its fur was a million shades of gray tipped with white, and its tail was very squirrel-like in its carriage, length and fluffiness. She created a new slot in the animal kingdom for this enigma, and called it a "Squear (pn. Squ-are)," – the natural result of crossing a squirrel with a bear -- then immediately cast about for the presence of a possibly-over-protective, people-eating mother squear.

With relief, Alisha concluded that the two seemed to be alone.

Alisha lowered herself slowly to a sitting position and picked up a twig, to which she gave an inordinate amount of scrutiny. Seeming to feel less threatened, the squear dropped to all fours and sidled closer, also selecting a twig. Thus, similarly occupied, the two formed a peculiar twig-twisting team of sorts. There were plenty of twigs and all the time in the world in which to twist them. Alisha exulted in the lack of solitude that this fragile alliance provided.

It wasn't long before the twig-twisting had become a relaxed day-dreaming session. If her new friend was to be a "Squear," then what would a "Sur-call" look like? She gazed at the clouds for inspiration. As a matter of circumstance, she had reached such a high state of Zen that she had taken no notice when her companion had slipped quietly back into the forest – leaving her stunningly alone in a pile of twisted, wooden debris.

Alisha stood up and called gently after it. "Squear? Little Squear? Come back! Hello?"

She brushed bits of twig off of her shirt and jeans, taking note of a painful stiffness in her joints and the urgent need to relieve herself.

Skink

As with most things, Matthew had accepted his nickname without question. A "skink" was a small, striped burrowing lizard. He wasn't sure who had come up with this, or when, but had nothing against small striped burrowing lizards, so took up answering to it almost immediately and without argument.

The world had gone decidedly wonky since Alisha had failed to show up for dinner on Saturday. He had the utmost faith in his sister to survive most hardships. She was a bit compulsive on the topic of survival. Most people figured she was a product of too much television, but he also knew her to be a seeker of all things disaster. For example, if the topic of tornadoes was to surface in general conversation, she would excitedly volunteer every known piece of advice ever accumulated by human science. She would still be spouting helpful tips long after the group had dispersed to pursue other interests.

Self-defense? She had advice. Earthquakes? Tsunami? Volcanic Eruption? Nuclear Holocaust? Alisha was your girl. Of course, she wasn't immortal (yet). He supposed she could have been shot, stabbed, abducted by Aliens or wandered through a door to an alternative reality... So, he was worried. But, not anywhere near the level of hysteria his parents were exhibiting.

Sentry Heights Senior High had become "Alisha Central." The perks this represented to Skink were pretty substantial. The "Fab-Five" top-echelon of popularity and sexual attractiveness had taken him on as a media magnet and charitable mascot of the month. Being seen with him was all the rage. The local news affiliate had showcased his family's pleas for her return the last three nights running. And, he had to admit, the Oprah thing was looking kinda' cool.

People kept asking him "Did Alisha tell you where she was going?"

Um. Duh. There were only so many ways to say "No. I didn't drag my ass out of bed until I had to whiz."

He'd come up pretty short when it came to an "alibi," because of it, too. Apparently, there had been no witnesses to his laziness and total lack of motivation. Things got better once the whole family had passed lie-detector tests. That was a radically cool experience, actually. So they were moving about without an FBI escort these days. Like he'd kill his big sister? Why? She had so rarely come out of her room, the thought had never crossed his mind.

He supposed that, if she had been like Bruce's sister, the naggy, bitchy, "I'm going to tell on you," type, well, maybe then... But, taking a dislike to Alisha would have taken a considerable effort on his part with zero-to-nil rewards. Without skinning a dead pickle, "It takes two to fight." Neither one of them had the stomach for it.

Pretty quick, Mrs. Weaver had come forward saying that Alisha had paid her admission fee and gone through the maze that Saturday morning. She turned out to have been the last one to see Alisha alive. Mrs. Weaver had passed her lie-detector test, too. But, not until after it had been revealed that she was having a steamy affair with the guy who ran the tractor for their hay rides. Probably screwed that family up royally.

Alisha would've hated that. She liked the Weavers.

The ensuing police investigation had pretty much annihilated the corn maze, anyway. A crime lab somewhere was probably up to its adenoids in husk fragments and clothing fibers that represented snagged clothing from every kid in town. As far as he knew, no trace of Alisha had yet come to light.

No. Panic was not his first choice of action. Skink kept up his positive vibrations by spending as much time as possible buried up to his elbows in Alisha's crappy Pontiac. It was an impossible task, really, trying to resurrect that Catalina. It was badly rusted out, and had a cracked engine block (for chrissakes). But, you just never knew where parts could turn up nowadays. However, with the advent of the internet – all things were possible.

Skink had a knack for acquiring the most sought after car parts. As a result, he was always in a position to trade. "Better than money." he would mutter as he placed another rare find among his shelves of inventory. Now, all that was needed was to trade down for some Pontiac bits, and he felt certain that he'd have that poor excuse for a rattletrap up and running in no time.

He gave the bowels of the Catalina one more baleful glance and then headed into the house for some Coke. It had been plenty cool enough in the garage, but he'd worked up a powerful thirst just the same. His shoes got kicked aside in the mud room (rules), and he cut left towards the kitchen before pulling up to a complete stop and changing directions.

Skink's mother was at the kitchen table with that unbearable 'look' on her face. Her dark brown hair was rumpled and dirty. The normally attractive layers of her short bob stuck up in impossible spikes and snarls – more the look of a punk rocker with too much 'product' worked through. Her eyes, a sparkling darkest blue, were no longer visible through her tear-streaked and swollen lids. Observing her as he was, from a safe distance, he thought that she looked smaller, more fragile than he'd ever seen her. He was overcome with a need to escape.

Honestly, it was hell to see her in such a state. But Skink had never been one for 'people skills.' He was expected to hug her – that, and to whisper some words of hope. But, Skink knew that his mothers' grief was a bottomless vortex that sucked people in and left them defenseless. All of that raw emotion was embarrassing, and made him feel antsy. So, Skink avoided the pull of those currents with all of his might. People could say that his lack of empathy was appalling (and often did), but Skink was Skink, and he had his reasons.

Somebody had to finish Alisha's car. Somebody had to be standing strong when Alisha came home. It wasn't in his nature to give up hope – not with cars – not with anything.

Busy Hands

Alisha gathered enough corn to get her through a few more days and bent some adjacent saplings to start construction on her lean-to. All of the ones she had seen on "Survivor" had been made with braided and interlaced palm fronds. She didn't have those, and wondered if the cornstalks would be a helpful substitute? The end result wouldn't be water-proof, but, maybe with a mixture of clay and husks jammed into the cracks?

"Well, at least it will give me something to do." She said aloud.

This reality wouldn't be nearly so creepy if there were bugs buzzing, or fish swimming by. What would she give to see a rat or a snake now? The squear had been her only companion, and his departure had left her feeling depressed and alone. Were there any other squears out there?

"There must be." She thought. "I wonder what they eat?"

As she harvested the corn, stalks and all, Alisha

considered the squear. It had been about 2' high when it stood on its hind legs. The creamy underside and silver coat had reminded her of a common squirrel, but the rounded ears, protruding snout, and black nose were more reminiscent of a bear. It was the hands that had been the oddest characteristic. They were furry, yes, but had nails – not claws – and an opposing thumb? His tail was gorgeous, and she noticed that his emotions were much easier to read if you took its movements into consideration. This creature was too small to have planted the fields. It hadn't made a single sound, either.

Alisha shook that thought from her head. "I'm tired and hungry." She forgave herself. "The squear was a cute little critter, and nothing else. I haven't launched myself into Narnia, after all. If that had been the case, I could've hitched a ride on Aslan and been home by now."

But, where was she? Why weren't there any living things here? As much as she hated mosquitoes and creepy crawly things, the complete absence of them had been a constant source of concern.

If anyone reading this has ever attempted to wrest a cornstalk from the ground, by hand, you'll perhaps understand why the work was slow and hard. Alisha's hands became bloody and blistered, not to mention the hundreds of tiny papercuts she received from the husks – which were all in varying degrees of decay. She had given up on the flip-flops. Whatever protection they gave to the soles of her feet was small in comparison to the skin they took off between her toes.

Alisha tried to do her work quietly, even though there was nobody around to hear her. The air was as full of threat as it was of silence, and she couldn't shake the feeling that she was being watched. As she cleared each armload, she carried them sullenly back to "camp." The temptation was to weave a few into place right away, but she knew it would go faster if she completed one task at a time. Her to-do list went like this:

1. Gather cornstalks
2. Separate out the ears of corn from the husks and stalks
3. Create rope by splitting the husks and tying them together
4. Secure a frame to the four saplings
5. Secure cross beams to the frame
6. Weave stalks through frame and cross beams
7. Dig for clay.
8. Mix fibers from remaining husks to make mud

daub

9. Fill all cracks in finished frame

"Gather all of your supplies. Do one step at a time. Focus on your goal." She could almost envision her brother's serious face as he had imparted this wisdom.

If Skink was working on a car, for instance, he would first make sure he had all of the parts. Alisha had watched him do this – many times – and he would tell her how important it was to do each task in a certain order, so that you would never have to undo anything just to get at something else. "How many times," he had joked, "have I watched the guys in shop class figure out that they have to pull apart work they have just finished to get to something underneath?"

The one goal she had not yet attempted was fire. She didn't wear glasses, carry a mirror, or matches or a lighter. That left sparks from flints, and rubbing sticks together. She wasn't holding out much hope on that score. As the day wore on, she grew more and more despondent. Her hands and feet were bleeding through a fine crust of dirt. She was thirsty and hungry and ready to go home.

"Home." She sighed deeply. But, it wasn't built yet.

By the time she had stopped for the night, there was a

formidable stack of building supplies to sort through in the morning. Too tired to worry about parasites and bacterium, she stripped naked and lowered herself into the deepest part of the stream (which was only about three feet deep) to wash. The water tasted clear and sweet, and she drank deeply. This tasted so much better than the muddy water that had been made "safe." If she was going to regret it, she would have to regret it later on. For now, there was just the healing water moving gently past her and carrying away all of the dirt and sweat and blood of a long day.

Alisha sat on the pebbled stream floor and bent forward enough to dunk her head in the water. Lifting it up, she parted her hair and swept the water away from her eyes with her hands. As soon as she could see again, she turned towards her encampment to see a squear watching with her interest. Was that "Her" squear or another?

They both stared without moving for a full minute before Alisha crossed her hands in front of her breasts and tried to stand up. Without her hands to assist her, Alisha fell backward into the water with a loud splash and came up gagging.

On the shore, the little squear slapped one hand over his eyes and laughed.

Alisha spluttered and wiped to clear her eyes. At the sight of the laughing squear, she looked down at herself and, realizing how ridiculous she must appear, joined him in his merriment.

"So, you think this is funny?" She asked the little animal. "I could have drowned in there!"

But, she continued to laugh as she rose up, naked, and slogged back to shore. She had given up on any attempt at modesty. After all, wasn't the squear naked? As Alisha approached, the squear backed up to a safer distance, but made no effort to escape. It watched her with sparkling eyes – full of inquisitive humor. While she dressed, it sat peeling a twig as though waiting for her to join in.

Alisha sat as close to the squear as she dared, and gathered a small pile of twigs which she positioned between the two of them. The squear seemed to take this in stride, and was soon lifting his twigs off of the shared supply.

"Do you speak?" She asked, never taking her eyes off her work. There was no reply. "Do you understand what I am saying?" Again, no reply.

Alisha ventured a glance at the squear, only to catch it checking her out in the same fashion. She laughed. "Caught you!"

The animal coughed. Alisha took the burst of sound for an abashed giggle, and decided to put down her twig, and reach out, gently, to take the squear's project from its hands. Before she knew it, the twig had been surrendered to her and the two had arrived at some kind of a miraculous impasse. Their eyes met, and a tenuous friendship glimmered between them as fragile as a thread of saliva from a sleeper's lips to his pillow.

Then, no longer complete strangers, they watched the sun set within the rippling mirror of the stream.

Cheyenne Name

As easily as the squear (it was a male squear, Alisha had been able to surmise) had taken up the task of peeling twigs, he came also to be of great usefulness in many stages of the building of her shelter. Whether or not he understood her motivation, he seemed to enjoy the singular nature of the tasks. They worked together in companionable silence – seldom touching one another except by accident. Alisha lived in constant fear of scaring him off.

As they worked, she began to notice that he sometimes hummed simple tunes to pass the time. There had not been a single word out of him, however, and she wondered whether or not he was capable of any kind of speech. His laughter was clearly that – neither deep, nor high, but with a definite "Ha, Ha" quality. Once, when Alisha felt she had caught enough of the tune, she would hum along. The first time she had done this, he had stopped humming immediately, as though he was ashamed at being caught out. But, as they became more and more accustomed to one another, the humming was less and less of an issue.

Alisha knew that sleeping under a pile of leaves and bark would help to warm her, and that had been easily accomplished. Ordinarily, she would have been put off by the possibility of bugs, but... well, this world did have some advantages. The squear had made a nest of twigs and leaves in the branches of an immature tree within sight of the camp.

Each night, the weather grew colder. It was hard not to notice the cuddly, softness of the squear. Alisha hoped that one night soon, he could be persuaded to sleep with her so that they could keep each other warm. It was her fear of scaring the little creature away that prevented her from proposing such a thing. Cold was bad, but the concept of isolation was... unbearable. No pun intended.

Later, while weaving the stalks onto the shelter's frame, Alisha thought about giving her squear a name. It hadn't seemed necessary, as he had been the only creature around. But, as she watched him waddle to and from the pile of stalks with such great earnestness, she knew that they had become a team, and it was time for him to have his own name.

All of the usual names came to mind; Rex, Spot, Rover,

Max, Buddy, Rocky, but they just didn't have the right fit. Lots of dogs were named "Bear," she mused, but that wouldn't do. Nope. She needed something exotic and befitting to his unique and semi-magical status. Alisha's Grandmother had been half Cheyenne Indian. She knew that their word for "bear" was "ahqui."

Liking the idea of that, Alisha tried it out loud. "Ah-kwee."

"Yes." She sat on her bottom and dropped her forehead onto her knees. "Yes. Yes. Ahqui it is."

Alisha knew that the time had come for her to act out the universal "me – Tarzan / you - Jane" introduction. So, she moved to face the expectant squear. Not knowing what else to do, she pointed to herself and said, "A-lish-a." As he was still paying close attention, she directed her pointing finger at him, and said, "Ah-kwee?"

Alisha didn't know what she had been expecting. They looked at each other for a bit. Him, squatting across from her with strips of corn husk in each hand and his head tilted comically to the right, and her, trying so hard not to be frustrated with the total futility of this one-sided conversation. Alisha had been just about to raise the curtain on a repeat performance when the squear pointed one furry finger at her and spoke.

"Err-ish-err."

"No way!" She exploded in his direction, "Are you kidding me? Did you just say my name! No f-ing way!"

The force of her enthusiasm sent him scurrying backwards. He cowered, dropped to all fours, and made as if to run – keeping his widened eyes on her to see what the crazy human was going to do next.

"No! No, Ahqui." She said, softly, wrapping her arms around her knees and resting her chin on top. "Don't be scared. I didn't know you could do that. I am so happy. You are very smart."

As the squear began to relax his stance a bit, she said: "A-lish-a" and pointed at herself with a big smile.

"Err-lish-err." He repeated, sinking to sit at the base of a tree.

"Ah-kwee," she pointed at him, pronouncing the name with care.

He pointed to himself, smacked his lips a few times, and tried, "Errgree?"

It took everything she had to resist laughing at the silly expression this effort had left on his face. His muzzle had frozen into a sideways grimace when making the "gree" sound, and his wide eyes had been searching hers for approval at the same time. The resulting image was priceless. Alisha thought this might be the funniest thing she had ever seen, but she hadn't dared to laugh.

"Close enough." She smiled. "Close enough."

Heat and Light

"Fire." Alisha said, aloud, with her hands on her hips the third morning. "Today, we are going to have a fire, if it kills me."

She rummaged around for a stick that had enough elasticity to string for a bow. Then, having found one that was suitable, she set about making the strongest string she could. Nothing worked! It was one thing to tie stalks to a frame, but quite another to create string that would possess the strength necessary to be wrapped around a stick and pulled back and forth with enough speed to create heat, sparks, and fire. All of Alisha's attempts at braiding, splitting, and winding the resources close to hand had failed, miserably.

Upon waking the next morning, Alisha renewed her attempts at making fire. Each time she had begun to see a tiny thread of smoke rising from the kindling, her strength had given up and she had been forced to start all over again. Angry blisters rose up on her palms and fingers, making each effort more impossible than the last. She knew that, eventually, her hands would toughen into rough calluses, making the work easier. But, it is hard to rotate the same stick for hour after hour without losing hope that fire will ever bloom as a result.

Through all of her exertions, the squear had watched her closely – first with his head leaned to the right, then with it tipped to the left. But, when she threw the stick angrily, and wilted against a tree trunk to dissolve into a shaking fountain of hot tears, he had scurried off into the forest at speed.

"No!" Alisha stood abruptly and hollered after him. "Please, come back! I wasn't throwing the stick at you! I'm not mad at you, Ahqui! Please?"

But, she watched, helplessly, as he went leaping and bounding through the undergrowth, knowing that she could never catch up to him. Alisha continued to gaze after him until the distant swaying and crashing of undergrowth had marked his passage to the edge of her sight and out of her life.

With her companion gone, Alisha's will to start a fire, or finish her shelter soon wilted and died. The forest had become too quiet, and only the sound of the leaves and the sparkling river making its way to somewhere else could provide assurance that the world was still turning. (If this world even turned?).

Alisha found her bed before noon, and buried herself deeply within the leaves.

"Pull yourself together." She whispered, staring at the dancing reflections on the water. "He was just an animal. You don't need to have an animal to survive. You just need..." But, the sentence trailed off to nothing as she, once again, felt the walls of isolation settling around her. It was cold. So cold that her feet were numb. Alisha had tried everything to keep them warm, from pulling her jeans low over her hips and tying the hems together, to curling into a fetal position and wrapping her toes in her hands. For the first time, Alisha thought she might never make it home again. For the first time, she began to wonder how she would die. Would it be from starvation? Hypothermia? Despair?

"He has gone away before, but he has always come back." She rolled onto her back, causing a leafy avalanche that left her chilled. "He'll be back. Probably in the morning. No point in getting all dark and dismal over it."

Ahqui's Quest

Ahqui watched the human, Err-ish-err, try to make fire. She tried day after day, but no fire came. Ahqui knew where to find the fire stones, but he didn't want to go to that place. She might yet make the fire on her own, yes? She was a very strong and smart human.

He turned his back to Err-lish-er and hung his head. Brr-ahn-ahh had been very strong, and very smart, also, but Brr-ahn-ahh had died.

Ahqui blinked twice and shifted his feet. Brr-ahn-ahh had come to this place to hide from angry Jurrahs and nurse his horrible wounds. Ahqui had been with Brr-ahn-ahh always and in many places. Bra-ahn-ahh had been the master for all of his days. That was very hard. The smell was death days before Brr-ahn-ahh died. The pain was bad. Brr-ahn-ahh had cried out often.

The squear grimaced and closed his eyes against the vision of his dead companion. The way Brr-ahn-ahh's jaw had unhinged and hung open – tongue lolling. He shuddered and wrapped his tail around his haunches. That was a bad, wrong time. Ahqui knew the fire stones were inside Brr-ahn-ahh's clothing. They had been tucked into a pocket for safe-keeping.

Ahqui turned to see Err-ish-err crying, and could sense the loss of hope that emanated from her. It was as though a door had slammed inside that locked her away from her will to survive. He had seen that happen before, and it wasn't good. Ahqui turned his eyes away from Err-ish-err and gazed off into the darkened forest that separated him from Brr-ahn-ahh's lifeless body. Err-ish-err needed the fire stones to make the fire. Ahqui would have to go and get them. He must go now.

If Alisha had been watching Ahqui at that moment, she might have witnessed a change come over him that brought a steely glint to his eyes and a determined line his mouth. But, all she saw was the swiftness with which he had bounded away, and all she had felt was abandonment and hopelessness at the sight.

Shelter from the Rain

Alisha awoke on the second day to find herself still alone. She rallied herself and set about finishing her shelter. Already, the lean-to provided protection from the coldest winds, but she knew that the roof needed considerable work before she could expect to have shelter from the rain.

She tied corn husks together and wove them to create mats for the floor and to fortify the roof and walls. Over the mats, she placed more stalks and secured them as best she could to the frame of saplings that anchored the structure.

The work absorbed her thoughts and had the end result of raising her mood, considerably. At each stage of construction, new ideas formed about how to extend and improve her shelter to include all four walls and a passable doorway that would swing open and closed much like a dog door.

The end result was a cozy, though very small, refuge that would make the bone-chilling nights less deadly. As the sun began to set, Alisha gathered some corn for her dinner and climbed inside her tiny fortress to eat and settle down for the night.

Just as if on cue, a gentle rain began to fall. Alisha listened to the fat droplets as they splattered onto the roof of her home and slid down a gutter that directed them into a basin-shaped rock nearby. She smiled.

Hours passed, yet no raindrops got past her defenses.

"I'm so smart, it's scary." She laughed. "This place isn't going to get the best of me. Any day now, someone (or something) will come after their harvest, and I will be saved. Until then, all I have to do is stay alive."

Alone in the dark shelter she had created, Alisha curled up to sleep. It was much warmer inside, but still cold enough to numb her fingertips and toes. Her thoughts drifted to her family, and her bedroom, and her books. Her mother was probably stirring some Manwich on the stove and Alisha could almost smell the sloppy joes and lima beans with butter melted on top.

They were messy sandwiches, but Alisha always asked for an extra roll to sop the over spilled meat and sauce from her plate. Her mouth watered, and she rolled over with her back to the makeshift door. Some people made their own sloppy Joe sauce with ground beef and spaghetti sauce, but Alisha could always tell the difference. There was something about the can of Manwich® that made the sandwich come to life in her mouth.

Alisha gulped down saliva and listened to her stomach grumbling and complaining about her diet of corn, corn, and more corn.

There had to be something else to eat. How could anything survive in this reality without meat, or dairy, or fish? Thinking about meat, dairy and fish was not particularly helpful, under the circumstances. Alisha bid herself to stop obsessing about sloppy Joes and just go to sleep.

As she drifted off, she wondered what Ahqui would think of the finished shelter? Would he come inside at night to sleep next to her? Would having him with her make this night warmer and easier to get through?

In the end, she decided that he would, and she dreamed of his return and their continued alliance throughout whatever was ahead. Those thoughts brought a smile to her lips, and might even have warmed her a bit, for she was soon fast asleep in her new home.

The Bad Place

Ahqui could smell the bad place from far away. It was hard to continue forward, when he wanted so badly to turn back. In the bad place, the creek had opened into a river that spilled into a lake. Ahqui began to recognize familiar landmarks and to catch remnants of his own scent amid the chaos of death smells that seemed to be reaching out to him from his own withered companion and friend.

Ahqui slowed as he approached the campsite. He knew what he would see, and braced himself for the horror of it. But, nothing could have prepared the little squear for the sight that greeted him. There, in the gathering darkness of evening, lay the twisted and broken body of his master. Brr-ahn-ahh's slack jaw had tightened into an eternal scream of agony, and his long, elegant, fingers had curled into angry claws that seemed to accuse Ahqui of some unforgiveable transgression and to demand revenge in the same heart-stopping moment.

To cry out, while a suitable and expected reaction in

human terms, was not natural to a squear. Instead, Ahqui froze into a wide-eyed, silence that threatened to hold him in its thrall for all eternity. His heart cried out from inside the tomb of his chest, however, it prayed for death and forgiveness and many things it hardly understood. The Pain was a living thing! His muscles pulled his tiny frame into a crippling parody of its live self, and would not allow him the tiniest movement.

In his mind, memories played on a stage of blood spatter and gore. Brr-ahn-ahh's voice. Brr-ahn-ahh's laughter. Finally, Brr-ahn-ahh's anguished cries of pain. Ahqui had been helpless to relieve his master's suffering. He had become paralyzed with fear of the writhing, gashed and eviscerated creature that Brr-ahn-ahh had become towards the end.

What would become of him? He had fretted. How would he survive in this strange place? How would he escape this forest of death?

A muscle twitched below Ahqui's tear-filled eye as he recalled, with shame, how he had longed for his master's hastened death! The sounds and smells of Brr-ahn-ahh's dying had become unbearable – nightmarish. He had longed to run from that place, and to see not one minute more of it – Hear not one minute more of it.

Now, Ahqui looked upon his master's tortured body with guilt. A thin whine escaped his throat as a trembling took over his body. The tremors seemed to release him from the frozen stance, however, and allowed Ahqui to move shakily forward – ever closer to his master – the witness to his cowardice and weakness in that time of such dire need.

But, as the little squear came close enough to brush the leaves away from Brr-ahn-ahh's dark curls, Ahqui was overcome with compassion, and the love that the two of them had shared magically erased the horrifying images cast by shadows, and returned his dear friend's features to their remembered form.

No longer frightened, Ahqui curled up under one of Brr-ahn-ahh's lifeless arms and fell to sleep, thereby finding comfort in the embrace of his forgiving companion one last time.

With dawn, Ahqui rose to find the pouch containing the fire stones in his master's pocket and he secured the silken cord around his neck. The water lapped quietly upon the lakeshore nearby, and he drank heavily from the still water before leaving that place forever. It was a long journey to Err-ish-err's side, but he felt certain that he could make it with a considerably lighter heart on the return trip.

The Gift of Fire

It was on the morning of the third day without him that Alisha awoke to find a robust fire crackling away on the riverbank. She rubbed at her eyes, thinking that she must have died in the night and awakened in heaven. But, even after rubbing her eyes and the pushing her leaf and twig-encrusted hair out of her face, the crackling fire remained. She was drawn to the delicious warmth pulsating from it, and the smell of the wood and cornstalks being consumed by it. Then, to her further surprise and amazement, she noticed the squat silhouette of Ahqui – holding his little hands up to the campfire for warmth.

"You?" She asked, not expecting him to reply. Then, (she couldn't have stopped herself), Alisha caught the squear up in her arms and mashed him to her chest. Oh, I thought you had gone away! I have never been so happy to see anyone in my whole life!" The little squear, shocked to be scooped up so unceremoniously, but happy to see Alisha's revived spirits, snuggled in to share in the celebration.

The fire was more wonderful than any gift she had ever received. Alisha held her hands out to it, and, once her palms were warm, she had extended her feet. "You did this?" She asked, pointing first to Ahqui and then to the fire.

Seeming to understand, Ahqui stepped forward and held out his hands to convey the gift of a small blue pouch. Alisha, puzzled, opened the pouch and poured the contents out into her hands.

"Flints!" She sat down right where she had stood and laughed. "Flints! You smart little squear! And, here I thought you had left me alone to freeze to death in this horrible place."

He is very smart! She thought, as she watched him proudly sitting in front of the fire. *I wonder where he found these flints? Somebody must have taught him how to use them, too.* A shadow passed over Alisha's face as she scanned the surrounding forest. *Was Ahqui with somebody out here? Was that somebody watching her right now?*

Alisha stood up and brushed the leaves from her jeans. She tucked a tendril of hair behind each ear and walked out into the forest a few steps. "Is anybody out there?" She called, with the bravest voice she could muster. "Look." She reasoned, walking forward boldly. "I know you are out there, and I won't have anybody jumping out of the bushes at me when I least expect it! Come on out of there, right now! Hello?"

Alisha stopped short to listen for a reply, and whirled around at the sound of an approaching footstep. There sat her little squear – watching her with the most quizzical expression on his teddy-bear face – the tip of his tail, twitching spasmodically.

Alisha stood her ground for another minute or so, until she began to feel a bit of a fool. She and her squear were certainly alone, but not without questions and suspicions. It was clear to her that Ahqui had been trained by another companion, but had still somehow ended up alone in this echoing, lifeless, dimension with her.

They were going to have to find a way out on their own before the onset of winter, or they would die under the pathetic lean-to, without a soul on hand to say even so much as a prayer over them.

The Harvest

It happened one day in the early afternoon, as she had known that it eventually must – sounds of harvest were drifting through the trees to their campsite. Today, Alisha would meet the farmers of this reality. Voices, both deep and high, clung to the leaves that fell around her. Though it was a language unknown to Alisha, the rhythm of civilized conversation was as welcome to her as rain to a desert, or oxygen to a fire.

"Ahqui!" She whispered excitedly to him. "Listen! They have come for the corn! They are here! We're saved!"

The squear stood at his full height and sniffed. A thick line of fur down his back fluffed up with agitation. There was no doubt about it – Ahqui wasn't as happy about this development as she was. Their eyes met and held. Was that fear she saw in his wide eyes, or warning?

That question was answered by his next action. A hot stream of urine and loose chunks of feces puddled where he stood. This was very much out of his character. Up until that moment, his toilet activities had remained private and dignified. As she watched, Ahqui's whole being began to vibrate with attention toward the voices in the field.

"Shh. It's okay. I'll protect you." She murmured consolingly. "Come here to me. Come on."

Without changing the direction of his gaze, the squear backed into Alisha's waiting arms. His smell was unnaturally pungent, and she could feel him trembling electrically within her embrace. Alisha stroked him, gently and whispered sweetly to him until his fur had begun to smooth down around his body.

As she gathered him close, she wondered what these beings would think of the two of them – the dirty and wild-eyed girl from another universe and her fuzzy sidekick.

"We need a bath." She said, finally managing to win his attention.

Alisha hurried to bathe and smooth her hair with her fingers. The tee shirt and jeans were scrubbed and returned to her body while still wet. Thinking that shoes would be appropriate for this occasion, she washed her flip-flops carefully, and slid them onto her well-callused feet.

Ahqui was not accustomed to a full-on bath, but there was no time to argue the point. He was dunked and scrubbed and fluffed like a prized poodle before he'd had opportunity to raise much of a protest.

Her heart was beating too fast. The voices of the

Harvesters were still audible, but more distant. There wasn't any time to be afraid. A short walk on trembling knees with a horrified Ahqui in her arms would put them in the midst of beings that could offer friendship or imprisonment – or worse...

The flip-flops had become foreign to her feet. She stumbled often, but would not remove them. To Alisha, the shoes were proof that she had come from a civilized society. Perhaps the comical rubber footwear would buy her an extra moment of consideration. She could only hope so.

At last, the trees parted to reveal a changed landscape. The fields lay before them – reduced to rough stubble and clouds of dust. Ahqui's legs were astride her abdomen, supported by one forearm. Her free arm cradled his back and held his fuzzy head against her shoulder like an infant. As she walked, Alisha kept up a constant whisper of encouragement though he continued to tremble, uncontrollably. As frightened as the little creature was, he had turned his fate over to her. She prayed that she was doing right by him – by both of them.

Human-like creatures gathered in small clusters up ahead. Carts were piled high with the harvest, and were harnessed to pairs of yellow oxen. The people-y things were short, dark and bald – wearing rudimentary clothing of varying shades of green and brown. A male and female turned as

Alisha approached and eyed them with suspicion and alarm. Many were clutching farming implements and scythes that glinted threateningly in the sun.

Alisha stopped a few yards away and lifted a hand in greeting to the nearest pair. "Hello." She ventured, meekly.

As soon as the greeting had left her lips, however, an ear-piercing screech went up from the female that was promptly echoed across the fields by a thousand voices. The chorus was so loud and unexpected as to cause Alisha to jump nearly out of her civilized shoes. Ahqui took that opportunity to scrabble frantically for freedom, and Alisha grimaced as she endured scratches from his wildly peddling hind legs and thrashing arms.

But, fully aware that her options were limited, Alisha had fought to quiet herself and her charge. She clasped him tightly to her chest and prepared to stand firm for as long as she had to. She was determined to establish a relationship with these noisy people-y things, and this was not the time to back down.

Then, off to her right, about a hundred yards away, Alisha watched as one of the males crossed to a large, red rock and pressed his hand to it. In that instant, they all vanished! Their screeching had been cut off mid-screech. Every single people-y thing was gone, and all that remained was an endless expanse of blonde corn stalk stubble and dust.

Alisha lowered Ahqui to the ground at her feet. Like one in a trance, she started towards the rock. About halfway, she discarded the flip-flops – one foot at a time. The newly-cleared field was like a million wooden spears of varied lengths and angles, just waiting to slice her unprotected feet and trip her up. Ahqui recovered the shoes without being asked and followed at a safe distance. Her eyes were on the rock. His eyes were on her.

"Is that the portal, Ahqui? Is that how I get back home? Can I go home now, Ahqui?" She whispered these words like a mantra as her destination squatted obstinately before her – now only steps away.

The rock was the kind of red you only see in Arizona. It was five feet tall and no more than that in width. Alisha held her breath as she circled slowly around, examining each craggy feature with a discerning eye. Had she come across it on her own, she would have thought nothing of it. She stopped then; her eyes had skimmed the rock's surface for any sign of a panel or button. Nothing. Where had the people-y thing touched it? Alisha looked back from where she had come and tried to gauge his relative position at the moment everything went "Poof!"

Alisha felt her fuzzy Sgt. at Arms tug on her left hand. She lowered her eyes to his, as if thinking of him for the first time in days. "Ahqui," she whispered. "Where will this take me? Do you know?"

His little hand slipped out of hers so that he could raise both arms up to her in supplication. This was such a childlike act, that she warmed from belly to smile as she scooped him back up into her arms.

"What should we do?"

Ahqui fixed Alisha with a serious gaze, and lifted one hand to point back towards where they had come. "Err-ish-err."

Mama Bear

Approximately one mile away from an incongruous red rock formation in a faraway land called "Maryland," Alisha's mother, Carolyn Ann Whitley, struggled with the child-proof lid on her bottle of sedatives. Her bedroom had been rendered dark at mid-day, and she had become one with the rumpling waves of bed linens and pillows – For days, only conscious long enough to seek more oblivion. The irritating lid finally gave way and Mrs. Whitley tapped two blue pills into her palm and gulped them, dry.

"My baby is gone."

There it was. She winced. That was the thought she had been running from – the one she couldn't bear to think.

"Alisha."

Carolyn Whitley collapsed back into the bed with thousands of unwelcome images assaulting her eyelids. Alisha at one – taking her first steps; Alisha's ballet recital; Alisha eating waffles; Alisha curled up with a book…

"No! Not my baby. Not my baby girl. I can't stand it. I

can't. I just can't" She cried out with such anguish that her husband, Grant, slid through a newly-opened crack of light to check on her.

"Honey?" His voice was hesitant, worried.

"Oh, God. Tell me they've found my baby? Grant, I can't do this. I just can't lose my baby girl."

He settled onto the bed next to her and lifted the prescription bottle to his eyes as if to see how many pills were left. Then he set it down, gently, and pulled Carolyn close so that her tears would fall onto his white cotton shirt. With one hand, he cradled her head to his chest and began to rock slowly back and forth.

"Everybody is looking for her. Everybody. All we can do is keep hoping that she'll find her way home." He said. "Carolyn." There was something in his tone that demanded immediate attention.

She pulled her head away from him and looked up.

"This is a horrible thing for any parent to get through, but, Carolyn, these pills aren't going to bring her back. The way I see it, you've got another 10-12 hours of La-La-Land before you're going to have to get out of that bed and put your big girl panties on."

His eyes held hers. She didn't look away.

"Now, take a swig of this lemonade and go back to sleep for a while. Start dreaming about how you're going to get up and start living again, okay? Because, your cruise to "Escape Island" is coming to an end. Do you understand what I'm saying to you?"

She accepted the sweating glass of lemonade and sipped. It was so sweet and cool. The lemons tasted like living things and bright afternoons by a swimming pool. She was thirsty – wondered when was the last time she had allowed any fluids to trickle past her broken heart. Carolyn finished the glass, greedily.

"I'm sorry." She whispered to her husband, actually relieved to cling to his strength. "I'll get up. Just give me a few more hours. I promise."

Grant kissed the top of her head, and lifted her chin with the fingers of one hand until they were looking into each other's eyes.

"I love you so much." He said. "We are going to be okay. We are all going to be okay."

The room went velvety dark as he closed the door behind him. She turned on her side and burrowed into the covers once again. In minutes, that velvet had enveloped her into a loving embrace and carried her – once again – into oblivion. Carolyn allowed Grant's words to follow her out of consciousness.

"We are going to be okay. We are all going to be okay."

The Rock

Alisha's head hurt. She needed to stomp down some of the stubble in order to have a decent place to sit for a while. Once that had been accomplished, she pulled Ahqui onto her lap and dropped her head into one hand. There was pressure behind Alisha's eyes that seemed enough to send the two orbs flying to the end of their stalks, and a steady pounding of her pulse hammering drum-like in her ears. If she had been home, she could have reached for some Excedrin Migraine. Unfortunately, Where the Fuck am I had no such item, nor a shelf to store it on. Alisha needed to think, and then the two of them had some serious choices to make.

"Okay. What are our options?"

1. Touch the rock and go ...

    a) Home?

    b) Wherever the People-y things went?

    c) Somewhere else, altogether?

d) Go back to camp and think about this for a while?

2. Touch the rock and take Ahqui with me?

3. Touch the rock and leave Ahqui behind?

   a) How much corn do I have left?

4. Will I survive the trip? Will Ahqui?

   a) Is it fair to take him out into an unknown environment?

   b) I should go back and get my flints

   c) I still have no way of carrying water

5. When should I go through the portal?

   a) At night, when more cover would be available

   b) Early morning, when visibility was best?

The questions assaulted her from all sides, but answers were nowhere to be found. These options created a verbal spin cycle between her ears that made it no longer possible to stand.

This was too far outside any experience anyone could have prepared for.

"If I leave the rock, will it still be here when I come back?"

It certainly looked solid enough. What if it was only a temporary portal? Maybe she didn't have time to fool around with plans and such. Maybe, it was one of those 'now or never' deals that popped up in fiction from time to time? If so, how much time did she have? Time enough to run back to camp for some food and her treasured flints? Her eyes looked back over the distance she would have to cross. How long would it take her to get there and back?

The hair rose up on the back of her arms and neck as an unpleasant thought crept into her head. "What if those people-y things are just preparing for battle? Are they coming back any moment to take us, or kill us, or eat us?" A new sense of urgency caused Alisha's plan to come sharply into focus.

"Ahqui? Go back to the camp and bring me the corn and the flints. Alisha will stay here. Can you do that for Alisha? Do you understand?"

His ears went back as his head turned towards the forest, and then popped back up to regard her. "Arrgree?" He pointed at himself, then back at the camp.

Alisha nodded. "Ahqui goes to forest and brings Alisha the rocks for fire (she struck imaginary flints together), and the food (she lifted imaginary food to her lips). Alisha will wait here."

He climbed off her lap and walked two steps in the indicated direction before turning abruptly on one heel and sitting on his haunches. He surprised her again by fixing her with a resolute stare and shaking his head in an unmistakable "No." Apparently, he had been learning from her at a much faster rate than she could have imagined possible.

When one of his fuzzy/rubbery hands took hers, Alisha crumbled to his will. She rose up and pulled him into her arms for the long walk ahead. Her pitiful flip-flops lay abandoned at the base of the rock like a poor offering to an angry god. And, in this way, Alisha and her best friend embarked on, yet another journey together.

Sleepless in "Where the Fuck am I?"

('WTFAI')

Alisha and Ahqui arrived 'home' during the early evening, and made fire their first priority. It was cold, and getting colder. The flames leapt up at the first spark of the flints, seemingly eager to welcome them back, and the light and warmth they provided made everything seem so much more possible. Alisha gazed at Ahqui's silvery form curled up and fighting sleep at the edges of the capering firelight and wondered how she had ever been able to survive without fire? Without him.

Back in her reality, Alisha hadn't been allowed any animals. (Her mother was allergic). Not even a puppy or a kitten – certainly not a rodent of any kind. As a little girl, she had ridden a hobby horse throughout the neighborhood, and exulted in its speed, muscular frame and luxuriant mane... (it had been a broomstick with a head fashioned out of one of her Dad's cast-off socks to which her mom had added a scraggly mane of pink and yellow yarn). That noble steed had been brushed and watered, daily, and you can bet that the bridle and reigns (twists of black ribbon) had been hitched religiously to any one of ten "hitching" posts when not in use.

Alisha had ridden a real pony once at a friend's birthday party. It had been a brown and white pinto, and it hadn't smelled all that great. Alisha had romanticized the experience later that day in her journal, writing that "The pony knew I was different from the other kids. We made friends, and he let me pet his nose afterwards." The more mature and sleepless Alisha laughed to recollect the steaming piles of greenish-brown manure the pony had dropped every couple of steps into its makeshift corral. (Probably due to the fact that it felt especially comfortable in her company). She laughed.

One Christmas, she had been given a "My First Puppy!" in its own special dog-house packaging. It could bark and walk (sort of), and, if you hit the big blue button on the top of the control stick, it could hunker down and pop up into an impressive backward flip. Alisha had scooped up the prized toy and run across the street to show it off to some kid whose name she has long since forgotten. Unfortunately, no amount of imagination could make the robotic puppy feel like the real thing. Once one had run it through those three tricks, one was pretty much done with it.

As Ahqui surrendered to sleep, Alisha continued to watch the steady rise and fall of his back. Her thoughts were chasing each other around the oddly-furnished and poorly-maintained club house that was her brain. Her experience with this honest-to-goodness creature had been worlds away from any of those early encounters. From the first snapping of the very first twig, Ahqui had been a source of hope and renewed spirit. And now? Now, they were more than a girl and her pet. They were companions, partners, and friends. Any thought of leaving him behind slid away from her like the moonlit leaves that floated past on the mirrored surface of the creek.

Alisha picked up a desiccated maple leaf and began to peel it free of its veins. What if she touched the red rock and found herself and Ahqui back in Maryland? How would she explain her absence to everyone there? What would her world think of the squear? She could almost see her brother walking around with Ahqui on his shoulders. He would probably think Ahqui was cooler than being on Oprah. And, well, it was... She smiled, allowing the fragments of the leaf to drop soundlessly to the forest floor.

It would be amazing to see everything restored to normal. Birds. Bugs. Traffic noises, and pavement, that dreamlike moment when she would cross the lawn to her front door. Mom would run out and grab her with tears running down her face... Dad... Would Dad be at work? Alisha tried really hard, but wasn't able to figure out what day tomorrow would be in her reality – Thursday? Sunday?

Skink would have finished her car. (Wouldn't he have?) That made Alisha's heart squeeze a bit. She had missed them all very much. Still, she thought guiltily, she hadn't spent very much time focusing on home. Survival had taken up most of her waking thoughts – while exhaustion had swallowed the sleeping ones.

Alisha hoped that everyone was okay. For the first time since leaving home that Saturday morning, she was homesick. It was hard to believe that reality could be as far away as that big, red rock.

"I must have touched it when I left the maze." She thought, trying very hard to remember ever having seen it – much less put her hands on it.

"But, I was anxious to get home, and I really wasn't paying attention." Alisha smoothed her hair back with both palms in irritation.

Alisha sighed and quietly crawled over to where Ahqui was sleeping to curl her body around his. She knew that she should try to sleep. They would need to be ready for anything tomorrow. Anything and everything. Her eyelids wouldn't stay closed, however, and her thoughts wouldn't stop shouting for attention.

Wasn't it more logical to assume that the rock would take them to the people-y things? Would it pop them into people-y thing downtown? You know, right in front of the haberdashery and the bake shop? "One thing I know for sure," she whispered aloud, "if one of them opens its mouth to screech at me, I'm going to be screeching right back! That was so rude."

The only experience Alisha had with portals was what she had read in sci-fi and fantasy novels – but, she had read an awful lot of those. A red rock portal might send you to dozens of locations and dimensions. It would all depend on where you touched it. Alisha felt certain that she could put her hand on the same spot the male peopley-thing had. The problem with that was that she didn't necessarily want to go where they went.

Another thought popped like a soap bubble on her nose and took her by surprise. Alisha sat up straight. "They all went. He touched the rock, and they all disappeared."

That wasn't the way it was supposed to go. Ask any

geek and you'd get the same answer – you have to be touching or holding the other person to get through a portal. Right? Harry Potter? Star Trek (well, if the other person didn't have one of those flip-phone-transporter gadgets)? Alisha rubbed the back of her neck before covering her face with her hands and heaving an exasperated sigh. They had just vanished, along with their carts and beasts and towering heaps of harvested corn. That simply did not compute.

It was late – or early – and she needed to sleep. The future would have to take care of itself. Alisha lowered to the ground next to Ahqui, pulled him close and buried her nose into the fluffy and musky-scented fur at the nape of his neck. Alisha didn't know what the future held for her on the other side of that portal, but she would not have to face it alone. Whatever happened from now on, the two of them would have to tackle it as a team.

Before very long, the squear's measured breathing had carried Alisha off to dreams of home.

Terminal Rock

They packed their few possessions into a sack of woven corn husks and drank as much water as either of them could hold. Ahqui had started out on foot, but allowed himself to be lifted above the treacherous corn stubble to ride the rest of the way in Alisha's arms. The rock was still standing in its place of little distinction, and they made their way to it slowly, reflectively, with Ahqui's eyes locked on the forest as it disappeared behind Alisha's shoulder.

Standing in front of it sometime later, they must've looked very lost and unsure. Alisha circled the rock again and again, searching for anything that might indicate a possible touch point. Finally, she came to a decision and pulled Ahqui close before reaching out a trembling hand and pressing her palm fully against the most promising crag.

Their eyes had remained tightly shut, so they were a long moment figuring out that nothing had happened. Nothing. The ravaged field lay about them on all sides and the forest still rose up in the distance. Ahqui shrugged his little shoulders in the universal symbol for "Oh well. What now?"

Then, a flock of huge, black crows darkened the sky and spread themselves, raucously over the field looking for leftover kernels. Alisha pulled her focus away from the rock face to stare out at the birds in shock. Birds? It was then, that they heard the echoes of voices in the near distance. Bustling. Talking. Was it possible that they weren't in the same place, after all, but a kind-of mirror universe? Her head swam with possibilities and a mixture of joy and sadness at seeing these encouraging signs of life, but sensing that she wasn't any closer to home.

With great care and utmost stealth they followed the sounds. And, yes! As they progressed further from the red rock, they began to hear the sounds of a bustling town full of those people-y things! A short trek to the top of a rolling hillside revealed a thick stone wall cradling dozens of modest homes with thatched roofs and round clay chimneys in a valley below.

"Shhhh. We have to go down, Ahqui. Winter is coming, and we will freeze to death without shelter." She took in his generous fur coat. "Okay. So, *I* have to find a better place before winter comes, or *I'll* freeze to death, Ahqui."

The squear seemed to accept this, as he then settled

reluctantly back into her embrace with a "Hmmmph!"

In the end, it was Alisha and Ahqui who strolled through the town gate just before noon to stand in the center of town square as big as life. Like a tribe of vegetable meerkats, heads turned in unison and feet shuffled nervously as the people-y things (PT's) became aware of their presence. Alisha braced herself for the shrill vociferation that was certain to follow, but the shock of their incursion was so complete that it left the poor things quite speechless.

"Hello." Alisha ventured again, in her meekest voice. "We would like to be friends."

She set Ahqui down and looked at the assembled personages expectantly.

After a bit more shuffling of feet, a male PT broke away from the group and started towards Alisha and Ahqui. He was just under five feet tall, dressed, modestly, in a forest green tunic and rust-colored pants, and more-closely resembled a root vegetable than a person. His skin was the color of unwashed potato peelings, and he smelled strongly of 'Eau-de-Mouldy-Grave.' He was, however, in possession of the requisite number of appendages to qualify as marginally human-ish-tic. The fully-jointed arms and legs of these creatures were twig-like with roots drooping off the ends where one would expect to see fingers and toes.

At the last moment, Alisha noticed that his black eyes were beady and lidless – like black marbles glinting in the sun. It was hard not to back away in horror, but Alisha held her ground and kept her frozen smile appropriately affixed. *(I will disclose that Alisha never quite got over their beady-black-marble-like eyes. She found this lack of blinking lids an awful distraction, and would forever have to struggle not to stare).*

"Womprerru." He said, and then added. "Contempero dees Womprerru."

His voice sounded more like a hive of buzzing bees than anything else. Yet, his posture in speaking was friendly enough.

Alisha had gathered up her courage and stepped forward to shake his um ... roots(?) An immediate wave of alarm moved through the crowd in response to her approach, however, causing Alisha to drop the hand to her side and back up, slowly.

Looks were exchanged, and the ensuing relief had been so palpable that, looking back later, Alisha felt that her decision to withdraw, peacefully, at that moment was key to her acceptance into the tribe of the Agrigars of Natalo. *(Though it must be said that they were many months coming to terms with the presence of Ahqui, for they had never seen an animal of his kind, and could not be made to trust in his cleverness).*

"Hello." She said again. "My name is Alisha Lynn Whitley, and this is Ahqui."

And that is how Alisha and her squear came to live with the Agrigars of Natalo I.

The Natalo Tribe

The Natalo Village was primarily occupied by the Agrigars – (or the 'Potato People' as Alisha had secretly come to think of them) – but, within that group was a small sprinkling of Jurrahs from a neighboring land who had been forced to winter in that province due to an early onset of cold weather that prevented them from crossing the mountains to their home.

Jurrahs were human, as far as Alisha could see. They had more prominent brows (even the females), and were substantially hairier, but were in every other aspect similar to her. These dozen or so creatures were also the first to make room for Alisha and Ahqui within their temporary accommodations in the Katsan (or Inn).

The Katsan was a one-story, rectangular stone structure that ran along the North Wall of the village. Inside were two gaping fireplaces, one at each end. Primitive bedding had been set up along the outside walls, with wooden tables and chairs taking up the center space.

Jurrahs were hunters, Alisha surmised, who regularly traded meat and furs for the crops grown by the Agrigars. As a result, generous portions of roasted meat were to be served at every meal, and warm furs were heaped luxuriously upon Alisha's sleeping mattress.

There was still a substantial language barrier. The Jurrah's were able to speak Agrigar fluently, but had never been confronted with an English-speaking teen from a faraway universe called "Maryland." They understood the basic needs of all living creatures, thankfully. The food and drink – though unidentifiable for the most part – was delicious and generously provided. At mealtimes the Katsan was filled with the mouthwatering aroma of searing fat – a smell not too different than that of bacon frying. It had been weeks since Alisha had eaten so richly, and she was ravenous.

Alisha had also been relieved to see that the Jurrah's menu met Ahqui's dietary requirements. Though it had been shocking for her to watch Ahqui tear into a slab of meat for the first time. She had always assumed him to be a vegetarian.

These questions raised her curiosity. Where had Ahqui come from? Had he been as trapped in that reality as she had been? It was true that there hadn't been any other living creatures in those woods – certainly, no other squears. The little guy had gotten by on corn, just as she had. Surely, if that had been Ahqui's home reality, there would have been other food sources available to him?

Sinking into her husk-stuffed mattress and fur coverings that first night, protected by walls of stone, was the closest thing to heaven Alisha thought she would ever know. She had been afraid, but she had done it – found a safe place for the two of them to pass the winter months. It wasn't home – but it would do for now. Alisha shuddered. What if they had not escaped "Where The Fuck Am I" when they did? Would she have eventually become a delicacy for Ahqui? Or – and this thought sickened her even more – would she have eventually been forced to eat *him*?

Unwilling to devote another second to thoughts like those, Alisha pulled the furs up around her ears and snuggled down further into the bed. Within minutes, surrounded by the hypnotic snap and crackle of twin hearths, and the comforting snores and whisperings of her fellow 'human-ish' beings, Alisha tucked her toes under the heavy circle of Ahqui's furry body and fell into a deep, uninterrupted sleep.

The first morning in Natalo brought many curious visitors to the Katsan. Some came to stare, and others came with gifts and offerings of welcome. The Jurrahs had absorbed Alisha into their clan as easily as dogs will sometimes be known to nurse abandoned kittens. The Agrigars were frightened, however, and Alisha had to wonder whether or not the gifts they brought were meant as a welcome or more as an offering to assure her continued good will?

Alisha's tattered clothing was immediately replaced with a tunic and pants of soft leather, and her flip-flops – though a source of much amusement within the Jurrah community – were placed aside in favor of warm boots. She was given a comb and a brush made of who-knows-what, but they were lovely and gratefully received. There was also a clay pot full of some kind of paste (she learned later, that this was the Agrigars equivalent to soap), and she washed in a rock indentation in the floor that had been made for that purpose and filled with buckets of water made hot by the fire. As a particular honor, Alisha had been allowed to bathe first, with the remainder of the Jurrahs following after in progressively colder and dirtier water.

Once clean and dressed head-to-toe in Jurrah finery, Alisha began to draw the attention of some of the young Jurrah males in the group. She was flattered, immensely, by the attention, but was never quite sure what it was they were saying to her. If any of the Agrigar males had an interest in Alisha, their unblinking eyes, strange appendages, and dank, earthy smell made it impossible to discern.

Wherever they went throughout the village, Ahqui insisted on being in her arms, or by her side. He was famously popular with the little Agrigars ('Tater Tots'), who gathered around him and ran their odd root-like fingers down his back and arms while making cooing sounds. He was the first squear anyone had ever seen, and the first animal of any kind that had been permitted to live, sleep and eat among them.

Cautious parents warned their children away from Ahqui – certain that he must carry disease, or that he had the potential to attack at any moment. Agrigar young, Alisha observed, were as children everywhere, and ran to play with Ahqui the moment their guardian's backs were turned.

Ahqui would get tired of this occasionally, but not often. Alisha knew when it was best to shoo his admirers away and pull him up to sit on her shoulders – well out of reach.

Soon the snow began to fall and gather against the town walls in drifts of 4 feet or more. Smoke drifted lazily out of every chimney – morning, noon and night – adding a fragrant incense to the crisp, cold winds that buffeted the village without ceasing. But, even on the coldest of days, Alisha and Ahqui could be seen leaving the village gates to walk the mile or more to the 'Ghama Traya' (which is what the natives called the red rock).

On some of these expeditions, they had been accompanied by a Jurrah boy who went by the name of Rhamas (*pronounced rah-mas*). Rhamas was tall for a Jurrah, and he was well known for his wide smile and laughing nature. Of all the Jurrah males, it was Rhamas who best penetrated Alisha's walls of language and inhibition. While several still considered themselves participants in the race to win her affections, Rhamas had established himself as the clear forerunner, and everyone knew it.

For her part, Alisha found Rhamas indispensable as a translator and teacher of both the Agrigar and Jurrah tongues. She hadn't done well with high school Spanish, so was surprised every time she had been able to come up with the right response to a query from one clan or another. In a matter of weeks, she had found herself picking up snippets of conversation and understanding, more naturally, everything that was going on around her. Along with this facility of understanding came a knowledge that she had been accepted fully as a member of the Jurrah race – with no distinction of other-worldliness hanging about her person.

As they crunched through the snow on their way to the rock, Rhamas told Alisha the many stories surrounding the Ghama Traya. The Wise Man of the Agrigars had learned to use it many years ago to access a 'like' world for the purpose of farming additional acres and increasing their wealth. The Agrigars referred to this adjacent world as "Natalo II."

"Not 'Where the Fuck am I?'" Alisha mused inwardly, preferring her name for the desolate place.

Only their Wise Man knew how to operate the Ghama Traya, however, and any who had tried to operate it without him had perished – never to be seen or heard from again. All knew the Ghama Traya to have great power. Most feared it. The Jurrahs refused to believe in such nonsense, altogether, but he had seen many an Elder cut that stone a wide path, just the same.

Though Rhamas tried to understand Alisha's longing to touch the Ghama Traya and travel back to her lost home, he strongly cautioned her against doing so unadvisedly, and offered take her to the home of the Agrigar's Wise Man to see if he would be willing to help her. Alisha had grasped onto that offer with much hope, but, though she had frequently reminded Rhamas of his promise in days to come, the visit had been postponed repeatedly with such a myriad of explanations and rationalizations that it led her to believe that Rhamas might have his own reasons for wishing her to stay.

The women of the Jurrah tanned hides and made clothing. Alisha found these tasks enjoyable, and took pride in her work. There was something peaceful about knowing how she would spend the days of her life. At home, in Maryland, she would have been attending boring classes in preparation for going off to college. There, the decision of which road to take had been overwhelming and fraught with dark foreboding. What if she chose a profession that she hated? What if she graduated college and still hadn't figured out where she belonged? Her Dad wanted her to follow in his footsteps and become a lawyer. Did she want to be a lawyer? But, if not a lawyer, then what? A butcher, a baker, a candlestick maker? The choices had seemed endless and yet all out of reach. But, here, with the Jurrah people, she was assured a life of quiet satisfaction – one in which she could take pride in her work and find peace within the simple fabric of an ancient way of life.

The Jurrah women married in their 20s and brought plump and hairy babies into the clan that were loved and cared for by all. Alisha knew that many expected her to marry Rhamas. This thought was not altogether an unpleasant one. He was handsome and kind – well regarded by both Jurrah and Agrigar alike.

As the winter wore on, each day took her thoughts

further from her life in Maryland. She began to convince herself that she had been ill-suited to life in that world all along, and, though she could still conjure the faces of her brother, father and mother, Alisha knew that her family had probably long ago given her up for dead. Why was there peace in that knowledge? Perhaps, being dead in that world, had granted Alisha the freedom to live on in this one?

It was in her dreams that Alisha longed for home. She often imagined the moment when Skink would present her with the glorious Catalina. In these imaginings, the car would start right up and sound like a new Ferrari. Skink would be leaning in the passenger window with a broad smile on his face, and she would be beaming back at him from behind the glossy steering wheel with an intoxicating mixture of love and gratitude for all that he had done to make the Pontiac new again – just for her. But, when she dreamed the bit about impressing the High School boys with her "ride," it was always Rhamas beaming at her in the school parking lot rather than the studs from the football team.

She would awaken from these dreams with a troubling grain of disquiet that stayed with her throughout the following day. Alisha was then made to wonder what she was doing with the Jurrahs in this foreign place, when she should be trying to get back to her home and family in Maryland? How was she now so far-removed from her goal?

But, like any disquieting thought, these were quickly forgotten in the reassuring tasks of each new day, and the warm and knowing smiles exchanged between herself and her practically-promised mate, Rhamas. The quiet joy of his arm around her waist, and the gentle coaxing of his mouth to pronounce each word and phrase correctly, filled the days, and her heart, equally.

Carried Away

The winters in Natalo were bitter. Many blizzards threatened to bury the village, and brought with them such winds that even the large, stone Katsan seemed likely to lift up and take to the air like Howard Hughes's 'Spruce Goose.' On these days, the Agrigars huddled in their cottages behind locked doors and shutters, boiling up huge pots of vegetable soup and counting impossibly large bags of seed in preparation for the coming spring and summer.

The Agrigars were a happy people. Though, if they'd ever smiled, Alisha had not seen it. The Agrigars were singers. They had a tune for everything, and an uncanny ability to start and stop songs in unison (by the hundreds). This music was especially enchanting as it came wafting up the village chimneys along with the delicious aromas of hearty soups and fresh-baked breads to join in muffled (cozy) unison above the snow and ice like a chorus of kazoos.

The Jurrahs often caught themselves singing along, as it was very hard not to. Ahqui had also found this hard to resist

– humming along as his ears, feet and hands kept up a happy rhythm. The Agrigar words were elusive, but that didn't stop a clever Jurrah here and there from making up lyrics of their own. (Often leaving the occupants of the Katsan in a state of helpless laughter).

Alisha cherished those times most of all. Alone among the Jurrahs she could bury the unease that the sight of the Agrigars had always stirred in her. They were friendly enough, even coming to the Katsan from time to time to exchange their soups and breads for meats and furs. She simply had never gotten over her initial distaste towards them. Their eyes. Their smell.

"I believe your animal to be possessed by a dancing spirit." Rhamas said one day, poking Ahqui in his furry tummy and catching a full-on ears-folded-back scowl from the squear in return.

"Yes. I have caught him at humming many times. He can almost make words, too. I have taught him how to say his name and mine."

"No, you have not done this thing!" Argued Rhamas, playfully covering Alisha's head with a white Corbus fur that she had been working on.

Alisha left the fur in place, peeking at Rhamas from underneath with her lips in a little pout. "You don't believe me?" She whined. "Me, your truest love and traveler from distant lands? How can you fail to believe me?"

Rhamas fell prey to her pouty lips in the same way that all men do, and pulled Alisha close for a tender kiss. Ahqui, with a huff of disgust, dropped from his perch on the seat of a chair with a "plop" and stomped (as well as any squear could) towards the hearth where the children were playing.

"Your animal fails to appreciate my greatness." Rhamas teased in Jurrah.

"No. But, don't let that worry you. He didn't want to come to the village in the first place. Perhaps, it is a mistrust of everyone who isn't me?"

Rhamas pointed to the laughing children who were happily fussing over the squear. "I don't know, sweet one. He likes the children well enough – and you are certainly no child!"

Alisha pulled her eyes from Ahqui's antics and found Rhamas's feverish gaze. He removed the silly fur from her head and pulled her close for another kiss. Alisha's body responded with tingling pleasure.

"Many say that we should marry before setting off in the

spring."

"Oh?" She whispered, their mouths still tantalizingly close. "And who are these 'many' you speak of?"

One hand carefully swept a lock of hair out of her face, as he answered. "Every Jurrah and Agrigar living within these village walls talks of the wisdom of this."

"And, you would marry me?" She asked, with the kind of coyness she had only seen deployed on dusty re-runs of "Petticoat Junction," and "I Love Lucy."

Alisha suddenly became aware of an uncharacteristic silence throughout the Katsan, and pulled her eyes from his to find those of every Jurrah turned towards the two of them in anticipation of his answer. Alisha felt the blood rising to her cheeks in a hot flush of timidity.

"Oh, yes! Alisha, I will have you as mine, or die trying." He said, with a voice loud enough to be heard from hearth to hearth. "Would you have me die?"

Alisha lowered her eyes and smiled with a kind of humble joy.

"Who am I to kill such a one as you?" She asked, laughingly. "I would rather torture your days and nights for many years than to cheat myself of such sport with your death."

The Katsan erupted in laughter and a general slapping of backs, and Rhamas stood to raise his arms over his head in a show of victory that brought a thrill of pleasure to Alisha's throat and wrists — wherever the blood could make its increased pulsations known.

It was in the middle of this celebration that Alisha sought out Ahqui. He stood by the fireplace with his back turned to the room — his shoulders, stiff with disapproval. This made her forehead crease and her lips press tightly together.

Why did Ahqui act this way towards the Jurrahs? Why did he wish to take her from this village and these people?

A cloud of doubt rose in Alisha's chest. What had she done? Was she truly ready to marry Rhamas and abandon all hopes of ever returning home?

The room was alive with anticipation of a wedding, and nobody took notice of Alisha's fallen mood. She rose to her feet and started towards Ahqui, moving through the tumult as if through a dream. As she came closer to him, Ahqui turned to face her with a profound expression of grief on his features. Alisha kneeled in front of the squear and pulled him into her arms as she had done so many times before. How had she failed to see this pain in his eyes, this sadness in the position of his ears, and the set of his mouth?

"What have I done, Ahqui?" She whispered into his ear as she rocked him like an infant against her chest. "How have I forgotten myself so completely? How have I failed to listen to your warnings? Tell me, little Ahqui, what makes you so sad that my heart aches for you?"

Alisha's was moved as his little hand patted the back of her neck in an effort to console her. The crowd of Jurrahs became no more than a fog of noise and movement outside of their perception. It was just the two of them, now; huddled and a bit lost, but still the lone stewards of an unbreakable bond.

A Fugitive among Them

It was mid-morning during the fifth (or sixth?) major storm, when the strangers arrived. They wore matching navy blue coats and high black boots. Nothing could be seen of their faces, as those were wrapped from the bridge of their noses downward with black wool scarves. To Alisha, none of those details were of immediate interest. It was their hats... They were fashioned from thick silver furs with white tips on the end. A fluffy tail hung down behind each. She pushed herself from the window with a sharp intake of breath.

"Ahqui!" She called, wanting him near. "Ahqui! Come here, please!"

The squear was not accustomed to being ordered about, and so he approached Alisha with a questioning look. Alisha wasted no time in scooping him up into her arms and turning her back to the whoosh of snow and ice that burst through the door of the Katsan behind her.

Loud greetings were exchanged, boots were stomped

clean of snow and coats were brushed dry before removal. Alisha listened to all of this with her back carefully turned to the three new Jurrah. She hated herself for being afraid, but somehow sensed that these men were dangerous. She knew that they had killed squears for those hats. Alisha had never seen such fur on any other animal. She hoped with all of her heart that they would secure those hats under their coats where Ahqui couldn't see them.

"Sweet One." Rhamas had come up silently behind her, and Alisha had started in terror. "What is it?" Rhamas questioned with concern. "You are frightened? What has frightened my Sweet One so?"

Not wanting to draw attention to their corner, Alisha kept her voice and eyes low. "These new men." She whispered. "They wear furs on their heads."

Rhamas laughed, heartily. "Why, of course they wear fur on their heads!" He said too loudly. "Have you not noticed? There is a blizzard knocking on our door!"

A laugh went up from around the room at his comment, and the new arrivals were offered a bowl of meat and a chunk of bread near the fire. The new Jurrah men were settling down to eat, but not without casting some curious glances their way.

"Rhamas." Alisha said, turning slightly away from him as though riveted by the landscape before her. "Please, love, without making another word – not one word – wander over to the door and take a peek at the hats they were wearing? Please. I think, once you've done that little favor for me, you will understand the depth and nature of my concern."

Rhamas stood, unmoving, with a befuddled look on his face. Alisha wondered how much more direct she could have been. She wanted to strangle him. She couldn't help thinking about how frustrated her mom had gotten with her dad under similar circumstances. Like, the time the heel of her black satin shoe had broken during a swanky company reception at the Kennedy Center, and she needed to grab him and slip out without being noticed.

As the story went, Dad responded to her plight with a booming voice: "But, why do you want to leave now? They haven't even served dessert!" What is it that makes men completely immune to our discrete hints and quiet signals? Why was Rhamas standing there like a block of wood, when she needed him to follow her simple instructions without upsetting Ahqui or creating a scene?

"Rhamas?" She asked, too sweetly. "Will you do as I ask, or will I be very displeased and unhappy with you?"

It was a relief to see him turn, finally, and walk towards the pile of coats by the door. He poked through them for a while before uncovering a section of the glorious silvery fur she had sent him to find. His head shot up, his eyes met hers, and Alisha nodded her confirmation.

A voice boomed from the hearth. "Ah! You have seen our beautiful hats! I'll bet you have never seen fur of such beauty? Am I correct?" The Jurrah had leaned back in his chair to brag, boldly.

Alisha watched, tensely, as Rhamas wheeled, smiling broadly, to respond in a similarly robust way. "Actually, I have seen such fur only once before." He answered. "But, it was being worn by an extremely close friend at the time."

Rhamas held the hat up for the crowd to see, and there was an immediate change in the temperature of the room. From a hearty exchange of news with hungry and well-dressed travelers, to a much cooler atmosphere of disapproval and unease.

"As a gesture of friendship," Rhamas said, gently. "I will ask you to place them in a box that will be stored under the eaves for the remainder of your stay."

The three strangers were dumbfounded by this

development. "What are you saying? Do you not wear fur caps? I see many of them here. How are we welcomed, and our clothing sent packing?" The speaker stood as if to fight and things got very quiet.

All eyes were on Rhamas, who was at that very moment carefully packing the offending garments into a wooden box and setting under it under the eaves.

Rhamas crossed the room to Alisha and turned her to face the visitors. As soon as Ahqui was revealed, the travelers gasped and sputtered in alarm.

"Honored guests," he smiled. "Please meet the woman I intend to marry! Alisha, these men are visitors to our village and will be staying among us until the worst weather is past."

Alisha nodded, politely, and, in perfect Jurrah, said, "I am very pleased to meet you. Also, please meet my friend and traveling companion, Ahqui, who shares our home and our food and our bed in this place. We would never have him feel the least threatened, of course. You must understand?" She looked from one to the next in a meaningful way.

"Where did you find that animal?" A second traveler leapt to his feet and demanded, rudely. His beard was so full that it started just below his eyes and continued, without thinning, down his neck to his chest. "We are hunting a Human who traveled with such a beast! He is a criminal and a murderer, and is to be put to death without hesitation! I will warn you now, that if you are hiding that human, or giving him aid in any way..."

"Sir. Calm yourself." Rhamas interjected with a trademark smile before the threat could be made. "My Alisha has had this fellow since his birth – a gift from her mother. They have never been parted for so much as an hour. There is no human here. We ask only that you refrain from publicly displaying ... er... Ahqui's distant relatives during your stay. Please sit down, now, and enjoy your meal! We will have no more disquiet tonight!"

The new Jurrah's exchanged a grim conference among themselves, before nodding and settling once more to their meals. Gradually, the house resumed its normal levels of easy conversation, burping, farting, and subsequent bursts of bawdy laughter. The female Jurrahs busied themselves with the service of food and the management of children as though nothing out of ordinary had occurred, but the glances that darted meaningfully between them told Alisha a great deal – nobody liked these visitors.

Alisha could feel Ahqui's nails digging, painfully, into her upper arm. His body was tensed, and she knew him to be afraid – even though he had never seen the offending hats. Not for the first time, Alisha wondered how Ahqui had ended up in WTFAI, and how he had come to be all alone in that desolate forest. It had been wise of Rhamas to say the squear had been with her since childhood. Wiser still for him to introduce her as his Jurrah bride, and not as the human woman that she was.

Could Ahqui have been traveling with the fugitive they were seeking? How had they become separated from one another? Whatever the answer, Ahqui's body language spoke clearly to her of terror and flight.

Alisha stroked Ahqui soothingly, and whispered softly to the top of his head. "I don't like them, either, Ahqui. I don't like them at all."

Ahqui looked up, and when their eyes met, Alisha became certain that her little squear had once been the companion of a human fugitive. Perhaps even a human male from her world.

The Wise Man of Agrigar

Alisha's Agrigar had improved greatly by the time the weather had begun to clear. She was, by then, able to ask most questions and understand most replies. It was a stilted and formal dialect, however, that required close attention on her part, lest she mess up a phrase and cause offense. Deciding it would be best to approach the Agrigar's Wise Man directly, rather than to wait on an introduction from Rhamas, she gathered Ahqui and set off to the other side of town to find his house on her own.

The Wise Man's cottage was grander than most, with a low garden wall and a decorative stone path leading up to its door. Even the door was grand. It had been painted a deep azure blue, and had swirls of paler blue decorating its border. The burst of color was startling to Alisha after so many months of wall-to-wall earth tones. Dazzling, even.

Alisha hesitated only a moment before knocking on the door, but held Ahqui closer to her as she waited for someone to respond. Just as she was about to leave, the door swung wide and a very short Agrigar in a jeweled purple robe stood staring up at them.

"Ah. Yes. You are Alisha, correct? And, this is your, um, creature? Yes. Yes. Do come in."

Alisha followed the opulently dressed Agrigar down a short hallway and right to a large, well-appointed room. She had not seen such furnishings since leaving Maryland, and was surprised at the quality of rugs and artwork that adorned the space. Unfortunately, no amount of finery could compensate for the moldy smell that weighted the air like soup. (To Alisha, this was the smell one would expect from a dead cat, firmly packed in potting soil).

"Oh. " She remarked, in what she hoped was flawless Agrigar. "You have a lovely home."

"Ah. Yes. Lovely. Yes. Thank you. I have picked up many things on my travels."

Alisha stood awkwardly, wishing he would ask her to sit down, but, as no such invitation was forthcoming, she shifted Ahqui to the other hip and began.

"I take it that you are the Wise Man?" She asked, awkwardly.

"That, I am." He answered in the rambling Agrigar

sentence that was required to say 'That, I am.' "But, you may call me, 'Ach Carush.'"

Rhamas had taught Alisha to refer to men of power using "Ach," as a prefix. She was glad for the reminder.

"Ach Carush, I believe that I came to this land in error by touching the Ghama Traya. Though I have been very happy here with the Jurrahs, and have made many friends, I would like to journey back to my home to see my family, and to let them know that I am well."

"Yes?" He climbed into an overstuffed chair that left his feet several inches from the floor. "And, you want me to use the portal to send you back?"

Ahqui struggled to be free, so Alisha allowed him to slide from her arms to the floor.

"Yes. I would like that very much." She answered, trying to remain composed as the little squear lifted and scrutinized some of the more costly accents around the room. "Ahqui!" she scolded, gently. "No. Please don't touch!"

"Well, I could do that, of course, if I knew which land you came from, and I had ever traveled there myself."

"I am from Maryland, Sir." She cleared her throat. "On the Earth world, Sir."

"Hmm. Well, I can't say as I have ever been to the Maryland Earth. What does it look like?"

Alisha was at a loss for words. She gulped what tasted like glue and ashes. It had looked a lot like a cornfield when she had last seen it, but...

"There was a cornfield that was surrounded by paved roads and shiny metal carts that could move very fast on quiet black wheels, even though there were no oxen to pull them. And, the houses were built of different colored boards that never needed to be painted."

"Ah. Hmm. I may have been there once or twice. It sounds familiar, in a strange way. Only, they had houses with vinyl siding and gasoline-powered automobiles with rubber tires..." He cleared his throat and directed her attention to Ahqui, who was, at that moment, attempting to climb an especially ornate floor lamp like a tree.

"Ahqui? Come here. Yes. Now, please." A dejected squear submitted himself to her arms where he began to rub his eyes and yawn.

Alisha allowed Ach Carush's sarcasm to drift to the floor. Her excitement at the prospect of going home overrode any amount of snarkiness Mr. Potato Head might dish out.

"Yes! Oh, Sir. Could you take me there? Just long enough for me to tell my family that I am well?" Alisha forced herself to breathe, as her heart now threatened to throb its way free of her ribs.

"I could take you in eight days' time, once the snows have fully melted, and the way is clear. Would that be satisfactory?"

"Yes. Oh, thank you!"

"Be at the Ghama Traya before the sun rises, and not one minute later. Can you do that?"

"Of course! This is wonderful, Ach Carush!" Alisha gushed. "I don't know how I will ever repay you."

"Thankfully, I do." The Agrigar Wise man leaned forward – His black eyes glinting nastily.

Alisha held her breath. *Here it comes. I should have known there'd be a roach in the Lucky Charms.*

The Wise Man cleaned his ear with one of the root-like fingers on his right hand, and then sucked at the waxy appendage greedily. Alisha was mesmerized. She hadn't seen anything like that since 'Grubby Greta' had harvested, chewed and swallowed the contents of both nostrils during kindergarten recess.

"I want the pelt of that creature." He gestured meaningfully at the sleeping squear.

Alisha felt the color drain from her face. Just that fast, all command of the Agrigar language left her. She swayed. She fought with her mouth to form the correct response.

"That is something I would never do." She barely breathed it. The shock of his request constricting her vocal chords. "Ahqui is my friend. We are never apart. I love him, as he does me."

The Wise Man waved his hand dismissively and slid from his chair to the floor with a thump. "Then you will never travel to Maryland of Earth, and I have wasted enough of my morning on you."

"No! There must be something else! Name your price, and I will pay it. Ask for anything else."

The little man ushered her to the door and shoved her through it. "It seems a simple enough matter to me. Get yourself another pet to coo over! I want that creature's fur for my pillow, and I won't accept anything less. Come back when you are ready to pay my price, or do not. It is all the same to me"

The azure door slammed shut behind her and a series

of locks and latches could be heard to engage from somewhere inside. Alisha's eyes stung with tears of humiliation. How could he make such demands and then put her out like the cat? That squat and misshapen potato head with disgusting manners had nothing to be so uppity about.

Ahqui stirred to wakefulness as soon as the frigid air ruffled his fur. Alisha patted him, absentmindedly and retraced her steps down the flagstone path, through the gate at the garden wall, and across the snowy village streets to the Katsan.

Of course, I could give the royal ass-wipe one of the traveler's hats, and problem solved. But, how would I get my hands on it?

Alisha's pace slowed as she considered her options:

1. Ask Rhamas for his most valuable furs and hides and attempt to negotiate a trade?
2. Steal one of the hats from the box under the eaves while the strangers were sleeping?
3. Make use of her feminine wiles to convince the ugliest of them to relinquish a hat?

None of those ideas seemed even remotely plausible. The unavoidable fact was that Alisha had eight days to get her hands on one of those hides, and she sure as ponchos on penguins was not going to touch one hair on Ahqui's body to do it.

Cold and distracted, Alisha fought to open the Katsan door, one-armed, before wrestling it closed behind her. All eyes looked up as each Jurrah in his own way huddled against the miniature blizzard that had followed her in.

"Vingtonah. No sutan consang, we tah?" Alisha apologized in Jurrah, which translates to: "Sorry. Nasty out, isn't it?"

The Closed Door

Skink had to go past it to get to his own room at the end of the upstairs hallway. He had to pass it again on his way to the bathroom, or downstairs for breakfast. He had avoided looking directly at it, and wouldn't even consider turning the knob to look inside.

Alisha's door had been pulled closed three days after she had gone missing, and Skink was fairly certain it hadn't been opened, since. It was as if her room had some kind of negative charge, he thought. It pushed you away – made you feel unwelcome.

Before that fateful Saturday when his sister had dropped off the face of the Earth, her door had been open around the clock. Alisha had been in her window seat with a book, or sprawled across her rose-covered bedspread talking to one of her dopey friends on her cell. Her iPod had played everything from the Beatles to Loreena McKennitt with the occasional show tune (played for the express purpose of annoying him).

Skink stopped, now, to lean his back against the door. His mother and father had gone out for dinner, and he was alone in the house. Alone in the hallway. Alone with Alisha's door. He had not yet shed a tear for his sister. Frankly, he had fully expected her to survive whatever awful fate had sucked her from the planet and come walking up to the house one day – probably at dinner time. He bent his head and smiled faintly.

But, she had been gone for nearly four months. He could tell that his parents were hanging on to a fine thread of hope, but the detectives were clearing their throats a lot, and the investigation that had never been 'warm' to begin with had grown cold.

"Are you alive out there somewhere, Alisha? Am I pouring every penny I earn into your crap-tastic car for a reason?" He spoke aloud, just under his breath. He was very aware of the feeling of his lips forming the words – very aware of the feeling of the door to her empty room pressing against his shoulder blades and hips.

"We know damn well that you didn't run away from home. Hell, nobody could ever get you out of your room, much less the house!" In the shadows, he sighed a humorless laugh.

The police had searched Alisha's room. They had

confiscated all of her diaries – she probably had a dozen, maybe more? What did she have to write about? Alisha never did anything. Never went anywhere. Skink wondered if the diaries had ever been returned. He knew that they had provided no useful clues as to her whereabouts.

Suddenly, the brother in him wanted to see if her diaries were in there. He might even read a few pages when nobody was around. Isn't that what brothers did? Read their sisters' diaries? Skink rolled towards the doorknob and draped his hand over it, but that was as far as his curiosity would take him. He knew now, with a certainty, that he could not open Alisha's door. It would be like pulling the nails from the lid of a coffin.

He shuddered.

"You had better be good and dead, Sis. I'm not kidding around. If you're gone much longer, I might start missing you. Really missing you."

Skink closed his eyes and thought about the time they had all gone to King's Dominion together. Alisha had been afraid to ride the roller coasters, and he had dared her to ride anyway. Alisha wasn't one to back down on a dare. Nope. She had ridden every coaster on the property that day – even the ones that looped upside-down. She hadn't liked the experience one bit, but she hadn't whined about it, either. He pictured the expression on her greenish face when he had offered to buy her that chili-dog at the concession stand. "Sure! Have 'em put relish on there for me, and extra mustard." She'd said, standing her ground like a bulldog. Skink ran his hand through his hair and smiled.

His body rolled away from the door and he turned to press his forehead against its painted surface. "I'm talking to myself. I'm big-time losing it, right? I'm losing it, and it's all your fault." A heavy sigh escaped his diaphragm and he straightened to continue down the hall to his room. Light flooded the corridor as Skink flicked on the switch in his bedroom, then quickly shrunk down to a fine strip that peeked from under his closed bedroom door. A television switched on and an animated gecko touting insurance chased the silence from the night.

The First Attempt

When Rhamas returned from his latest hunting expedition with his cousins, Alisha searched him out and welcomed him while making a big fuss over the abundance of their catch. He had beamed down at her with such pride and love that she caught herself wondering why she even wanted to go home again.

As his share of the bounty, he had garnered a large, white Canor pelt – which was very rare, as Canors are black with white markings as a rule. He pulled Alisha into his chest and whispered that he thought that the new pelt would make a very fine wedding tunic, before pressing it into her hands with a smile.

Alisha started working the pelt right away and, as she dried, stretched, scraped and treated it, she wore the bright smile and rosy cheeks of a woman in love. The Jurrah women teased her, relentlessly, but also gave her guidance on how to make the wedding tunic beautiful. These women would also call her to their fires to teach her how to cook the strange meats and vegetables found in Natalo.

Overall, this was a very happy time for Alisha, but there was still one spot of darkness hiding under all of that joy. She needed a squear pelt for the Agrigar Wise Man.

The oldest Jurrah in the Katsan was named Muanti. Alisha found that easy to remember because she had an Uncle on the Earth World named "Monty," and the two sounded very much alike. As Muanti was too old to join the other men on hunting excursions, he could often be found by the fire, smoking his pipe, or telling tall tales to the little ones. One afternoon, Alisha sought him out for advice.

"Muanti." She started. "Have you seen the fur hats of the strangers?"

He nodded. His eyes narrowed, as he had seen them and knew how much the sight of them had displeased Alisha.

"I would like to buy one of them, as payment to the Agrigar Wise Man for his help on a matter of great importance to me."

"What is this matter of importance, then?" He asked, with a voice full of age and smoke.

Alisha ducked her head and averted her eyes. "He travels through many lands with the Ghama Traya, and I wish to use it to travel back to my home."

The quiet stretched out for many minutes as Muanti sucked on his pipe and considered Alisha through narrowed eyes.

"And, how came he to name the pelt as a price?"

"He saw Ahqui, and how much I loved him. Only then did he wish me to kill the poor creature for his fur."

"Ah." Muanti nodded, sagely. His knowledge of the Wise Man was equal to such a bargain.

"But, as you have seen, the hats the travelers carry would suffice for payment and would not require the death of my dearest companion, Ahqui."

"I do not think those Jurrah will make a sale of their hats. That fur is very rare, and it brings them much pride. They are anxious to show them off upon their return to our village. I can tell you that they will not be separated from those pelts while they live."

"Can you see no way, Muanti? Will you think upon it a while? The weather is warming, and the hats will be on their way over the mountains very soon, as will I. I am worried that my chances are growing very few."

"Little Stranger, I can see that this matter troubles you.

Yes. I will think upon it, but I warn you, now, that your errand is more difficult than easy."

Alisha thanked the old Jurrah and went from him with a heavy heart. She knew that Muanti had been correct. Getting one of those pelts would take a death or a miracle. Also, she had yet to confide her mission to Rhamas. Alisha feared that most of all, because she knew he would be unhappy with her and also very threatened by the thought of her going away for any length of time.

Alisha burned with the need to share this dilemma with Rhamas. She could see that keeping the secrets could create a distance between them that she would regret very much.

"It is time to find Rhamas and tell him everything." She murmured to herself, wringing her hands and hanging her head. "This has gone on much too long."

Alisha knew that Rhamas was with the rest of the hunting party, making plans for dividing work and packing possessions for the journey home. Alisha used the time to wash and dress herself – even finding Tulahia (one of her Jurrah sisters) to work her hair into the traditional braided style of their people. Thinking, perhaps, that even as her words would not please him, her appearance might.

First Confession

Rhamas came from the men's meeting with a sour look upon his face. When asked, he told Alisha that many Jurrah hunters had developed a sincere distrust of the travelers who had come so abruptly among them. There had been rumblings and accusations surrounding Alisha and Ahqui, with many of the tribe having endured intense questioning in regard to her sudden emergence from the forest of Natalo II – holding that unusually tame animal in her arms, and then their subsequent arrival in the Agrigar's town square on Natalo I, shortly thereafter.

"They accuse you of hiding the human they seek, Alisha. They hold Ahqui as proof of this."

"Rhamas, I have no knowledge of any other human. This I promise you from my heart." She leaned into his side and accepted the arm that encircled her. "Ahqui came to me out of the forest, and I have come to think he was as alone and afraid as I. Perhaps, the human they seek found death in that world? I do not doubt that Ahqui was his companion – only that he was alone when we met."

Rhamas knit his dark brows at this news, and pulled her very close to whisper urgently into her ear.

"You must not speak of this to any Jurrah! The people love you, and have accepted the little animal as a friend, but no one wishes to be added to the traveler's list of accused, and nor must you!"

Alisha buried her face in his neck and nodded. "I will do as you say." She whispered. "I am afraid for Ahqui. They see his markings and cleverness as signs of his true identity."

"We must keep him close to us." Rhamas suggested. "Perhaps darken a spot on his face or back with charcoal to create doubt in their minds."

Alisha nodded again, then moved her mouth to cover his in a prolonged kiss. "Will the people help us?"

"As I have said, the Jurrah and Agrigars of this village fall onto our side of this debate, but do not doubt that they are being threatened. It is a very close thing."

"Rhamas? May we walk together to the Ghama Traya now? There is much I wish to tell you, that I cannot discuss in the Katsan."

"Sweet One," Rhamas replied in surprise, "There are

winds blowing that would carry the three of us to the doors of death and beyond! We will plan to go tomorrow, if Montaroon (the god of the Jurrah) will allow. Can your words hold until then?"

Alisha's disappointment was apparent, but she agreed.

Rhamas and Alisha walked through the crowded Katsan together where they found Ahqui among the women who were preparing the evening meal. The squear was growing fat on scraps of meats and cheese, freely given, that he could not refuse. The Jurrah people had fallen in love with his adorable face and impish personality.

Rhamas called to Ahqui, seated the squear on his broad shoulders, and the three ventured off to join friends in a spirited game of Hau Faycona Leia. They felt the eyes of the strangers upon them, and heard their grumblings amid the many voices through ears strained with a growing fear.

Rhamas is Wise

Rhamas was right, as seemed to often be the case. The sun had made a brilliant entrance on the dawn of the following day, and the air felt encouragingly spring-like in spite of the snow that still blanketed everything with drippy determination. Alisha gathered up Ahqui and, with Rhamas, they made their way to the Ghama Traya.

Alisha noticed that Rhamas took any opportunity to make sure they hadn't been followed out of the village. They made an effort to laugh and behave like the young lovers (that they were) strolling out to enjoy the first nice day of the year. Neither one of them wished to be caught outside the village walls by the man-hunters, though. Without witnesses, who knew what harm could befall them, or the little squear? For his part, Ahqui seemed relieved to be free of the village, and his spirits were higher than Alisha had seen them in weeks.

Once the party had reached the Ghama Traya, Rhamas threw a heavy fur cloak onto the snow, and gestured for Alisha to sit by him where they could talk.

"You have much to tell me, I'm afraid." He said, taking Alisha's hand.

"Yes." She set Ahqui down on the fur at her side, but the squear refused to sit still, and, instead, ran to roll and play in the mud and slush nearby.

"I am waiting with much patience." He touched her hair. "What is wrong, my Alisha, that we had to be so far from the village to speak of it?"

She bowed her head, and launched into the speech she had been preparing to make for days.

"Rhamas, I didn't want to wait any longer to talk with the Agrigar Wise Man, so I sought him out on my own while you were hunting." Alisha didn't give him a chance to react to that, but kept doggedly on. "He promised to take me to my homeland for the price of the pelt of my beloved friend, Ahqui, at the end of eight days."

Alisha saw the hurt in her love's expression and squeezed his hand. "I only wanted to go for a brief time. Just to tell my family that I was well, and bid them not to grieve over my loss, or worry overmuch for my well-being. Of course, I would return to marry you. That is what I desire more than any other thing."

Rhamas didn't lift his eyes to hers. He seemed to be deep in thought – wrestling with himself to find some solution to her latest dilemma.

"It has been my thought, all along, to get one of those wretched hats from the man-hunters to pay the Wise Man. But, think as I might, there seemed no way to make that happen. Now that I know about the suspicions that have been cast upon me and my Ahqui, the danger to everyone has grown too great. I must find my way home, Rhamas. I must see my family one more time. This is of utmost importance to me if I'm to be happy in my life at your side."

"Then you must go." Rhamas said, plainly. "But, not as you said, for just a little time. If you disappear suddenly, all will assume you to have guilt in this matter of the human they seek. Your return to me would surely become the end of you both. The Jurrah have no knowledge of the Ghama Traya, and will not know how to follow after you. It had not come to me as a solution, but, now that the opportunity has arisen for your safe escort to another place, it seems the only thing to do."

"How could I leave you for any length of time? How would I breathe? How would my heart keep beating?" Alisha could feel hot tears sliding down her cheeks, as she realized that Rhamas was sending her away, forever.

"Do not worry, little one." He pulled her close – her head resting on his shoulder. "I would journey with you, of course. We will give the greedy Wise Man three pelts, and three will make passage. If he fails to accept our terms, more's the pity for him. I am not a man to cross lightly."

Alisha drew in a sharp breath and lifted her head from his shoulder to survey his features. "You would go with me to my world?"

"I would go with you. I could not trust you to the company of this 'Wise man' who would bid you kill Ahqui!"

Though Alisha's heart was suddenly lighter at the prospect of going back together, she couldn't help wondering how she would explain her two companions to her family. But, the relief of having unburdened herself to Rhamas, and having a solution to her dilemma within reach, pushed all of the worry from her mind. She caught his eyes and laughed.

"You! You have taken every worry from my heart today, Rhamas. I am all happiness from here to here!" She touched her hair and pointed to her boots, and he laughed.

"This is what a husband does." He answered, looking for all the world like a full-grown man. "You should have brought this to me, right away, rather than worry yourself into knots."

"Yes. I should have. I promise that I will in the future – oh, wise and resourceful almost-husband!" Alisha grinned impishly.

They put their heads together then, making the necessary plans to secure the hides and make away before dawn on the day of their departure while Ahqui busied himself doing forward somersaults in the snow. They would tell no one of their plans. For this to work, they would have to make a clean escape and they would leave the man-hunters behind, cursing and scratching their heads.

"We will marry tomorrow." Rhamas announced as they approached the village on their return trip. At Alisha's exclamation of surprise, he continued. "We will be world travelers as man and wife, and that is my final word. We will tell the village that we are so much in love that we cannot wait any longer, and that will come as no surprise to anyone."

Alisha laughed. "But, I haven't finished my wedding garment."

"Then, you will be a very busy girl tonight, yes?"

"Yes, husband. A very busy girl, indeed."

An exhausted Ahqui clung tightly to Alisha, and she

brushed snow from his fur. *"We are soon off on another voyage, little Ahqui."* She thought. *"A very exciting one!"*

Their rushed wedding plans were announced that night over the evening meal. A cry went up among the ladies – for they had the most to do in order to make preparations, but anyone could look at the two lovers and see why they could not bear to wait another two weeks to be wed. Alisha enlisted some of her Jurrah sisters to help with her wedding garment, and the Jurrah men sat about – drinking and smoking – as men always seem to do of an evening.

That night, Rhamas tucked Alisha into her bed and kissed her, primly, upon her forehead. "Tomorrow night," He promised with a husky voice, "there will be no such kiss."

Alisha smiled and snuggled in as Rhamas crossed the room to his bed. Rhamas was her first-ever boyfriend. She felt all full of butterflies and warm honey at the thought of pulling him into bed beside her. They wouldn't have a bit of privacy in the Katsan, of course. She had lain awake on many nights listening to the lovemaking of other couples. All she could hope for was a ban on giggles and shouts of encouragement or instruction on their first night together.

Tomorrow, she would be a married woman. Alisha

wondered how that fact would be greeted by her parents. She could always say that she had run off to get married all of those months ago, and had only just decided to return?

No. Her mother and father would never believe her capable of inflicting that kind of pain on them in exchange for some guy. They would just have to be happy to see her, and Alisha could take it from there. It was one of many situations that couldn't be planned for in advance. She had encountered quite a few of those on her unplanned adventure, and had managed each to the best of her capability.

"Maybe that is what it is like to be an adult." She thought, drowsily.

The Wedding

Neither the bride nor the groom had been able to eat a crumb of breakfast that morning. Alisha had been bathed and scented with some kind of pollen and flower petal concoction that had been set aside for just such an occasion. The wedding braids were to be tiny and intricate and complex, and because of this, Alisha was held hostage on a chair by the fire while four unmarried girls tugged relentlessly on her hair.

Her wedding tunic had been worked on throughout the night, and was more beautiful than Alisha could ever have imagined. It was fashioned of pure white leather, with white fur cuffs, collar and hem. The Jurrahs had carried hundreds of tiny shells with them from the seaside, and her garment had been decorated with the most delicate blue and white ones that had been drilled and sewn on in traditional Jurrah patterns. Because it was a wedding tunic, and not one for everyday use, the hemline reached almost to the ground, with slits up both sides to the waist to show the white leather pants and moccasins underneath. As she waited, little shells were also woven into her braids so that she would catch the sun and glitter from head to toe.

Rhamas had been driven from the Katsan the night before, and was not permitted anywhere near her wedding preparations. He had been given space in the cottage of an Agrigar family nearby. Alisha wondered if Rhamas would be dressed in a ceremonial costume or would appear at the altar as she had always known him. She was very unsure of what to expect of the day, when it came right down to it. What if they sacrificed animals, or made her do a dance with snakes or something?

A tiny shake of her head (over the hairdresser's objections) helped Alisha to clear such thoughts and she occupied herself, instead, admiring the beautiful details of her garments. What would Rhamas think when he saw her all dressed up like this? She smiled and blushed. She couldn't wait for that moment to come.

"Are there pretty Jurrahs braiding Rhamas' hair?" She asked, to the giggling chorus of girls. "Will he have a wedding tunic, too?"

Kinstami, an older Jurrah woman, took pity on her and said, "No braids for Rhamas! But, yes. His mother has made a fine wedding garment for this day. You will both be very beautiful."

"Tell me what will happen, Kinstami. Please? I have never seen a Jurrah wedding."

Kinstami's leathery face crinkled up in a smile. "What do you think will happen?" She laughed. "You will be asked if you wish to marry that boy, and you will answer 'yes' – that is the hope of Rhamas."

A chorus of drums could be heard in the town square, and the girls put the final touches on Alisha's hair.

"It is time, Alisha!" They giggled, telling her that she was very beautiful, and they couldn't wait to see the face of Rhamas.

Alisha thought about her mother, and how her father was supposed to have walked her down an aisle. Things hadn't followed the planned route, she knew. She wiped a tear from each eye as she prepared to walk out of the Katsan and into her married life. Life happened spontaneously and had to be experienced the same way. Her mother would have to be made to understand – someday.

"Ahqui?" She asked, breathlessly.

"I've got him." Answered one of the younger girls. "Now, go! The drums are nearly finished!"

The Katsan doors had been opened for her, and Alisha stepped through them like a princess from another world. (Which, in an odd way, is what she was).

There was still a blanket of snow on the world, but the stone of the square had been made clear and dry. Alisha raised her eyes to look for Rhamas, but she didn't see him. Then, off to her right, standing like an archangel at the head of a long line of male Jurrahs, she found him. Rhamas's eyes were appraising her, and growing moist with tears. Alisha continued to walk towards him with measured steps, and as she got closer, her eyes followed suit.

"Damnation!" She thought. *"He's got me crying and it's going to ruin my face!"*

It was too late, though, as the tears had already begun to etch paths down her cheeks.

Rhamas was perfect. He stood there, tall, strong, yet vulnerable with love for her. His tunic was made of matching white leather, and covered with traditional images of good fortune in even stitches of blue threads. His shoulder-length curls had been pulled back in a thong of white leather and secured with an iridescent shell. Alisha's heart thrilled to know Rhamas would be hers and hers alone. Once beside him, they turned to face Moarti the Elder.

"I see many roads traveled within this union, and many marvels shared. The doors of countless worlds will swing open before you, with pathways unexplored. Wear this truest love upon you as a protection from any that might wish you harm. Let no road separate you – no quarrel render you unprotected."

"I see Rhamas before me." The old Jurrah placed his hand on Rhamas's right shoulder. "I see Alisha before me." His hand added weight to Alisha's left shoulder.

"Will you two become one, and vow to honor the covenant of my prophecy?" Moarti fixed his gaze on Rhamas, first.

"I join with her and remember your words, always."

The crinkled eyes found Alisha's next, along with his encouraging smile.

"I will join with him, and keep your words in my heart." Alisha gulped, her head down. *Had she said the right thing? Was it over now? What should she do?*

It was then, that the hand on each of their shoulders pushed the couple together so that they were touching – arm to arm. A cheer went up that was made up of Agrigar and Jurrah voices ringing throughout the village. Alisha felt

Rhamas's hand in hers and raised her eyes.

Rhamas wore a radiant smile that welcomed her to his love and protection for a lifetime. He turned Alisha, then – took her into his arms, and kissed her long and deeply on her painted mouth. Nothing had ever been so right. This marriage was the purpose for her detour into unknown lands. Alisha felt sure of it.

The noisy crowd faded from their minds. Alisha and Rhamas saw only each other – until they turned to find Ahqui being brutally wrested from the arms of the young girl and carried off at a run by the man hunters.

The Word of the Law

Grant Whitley was a tall man. He stood, gazing out the 19th floor window of his law office, admiring the floor-to-ceiling view that scared some of his clients half to death. He had to admit that it gave him the feeling of being in a glass-bottomed helicopter whenever he got too close to it. He turned his head to look at the stack of folders and documents on his mahogany desk. There was a lot to be done. People had been calling. Cases were pending. He crossed his arms in front of him and sighed.

In the months since his daughter had gone missing, Grant had been partially successful in convincing himself that she was still alive and would show up at the house one day – probably with some guy in tow. She would tell him that she was "in love," and that she had run away to get married in some po-dunk town where that kind of thing was still legal. Alisha was *seventeen*. Half the time, Grant imagined himself pressing charges against the jerk and ripping them apart with a sheaf of notarized paperwork, the other half... well...

Grant shifted his head slightly to see his reflection in the glass. He brought his fingers up to touch the gray in his hair. He observed many signs of aging on a haggard face, and tried to convince himself it was the light and shadow in the room that gave him that lost expression.

He wanted Alisha to come home - alive. He didn't care if she was married to a Yeti – to be honest. Two months ago, he'd probably have raised the roof, but now...

What if she shows up pregnant? He grimaced.

The phone rang, and Grant crossed, reluctantly, to his desk and sat down to answer it.

"Grant Whitley." He said.

As the deep voice droned monotonously from the other end, Grant dropped his head in his hand. He needed a vacation. He should dump all of his cases into Spencer's capable hands, grab his family, and take off for parts unknown.

"Yes. I can see your point. Okay. Fax the discovery documents over to Anna, and I'll look at them this afternoon. Of course. Sure. Someone will call you by the end of the week." Grant promised.

In the short time it took for Grant to form the sentence, "Someone will call you by the end of the week," he had made up his mind. He buzzed Anna's desk and, when she picked up, he said. "I need you to get hold of Spencer Hutton right away, and have him call or stop in. Tell him this matter is both time sensitive, and urgent. Oh, and get the travel agent on the phone for me, will you, Anna? Thanks."

A weight seemed to drop from Grant as he shuffled all of the folders into one pile and set them in the seat of one of the wing chairs in front of his desk. He wouldn't even ask Carolyn, he'd just show up with the tickets and tell them all to pack. Matthew could miss a few weeks of school. It wouldn't kill him, and everyone knew the kind of pressure they had all been under.

When the phone rang again, it was the agent, and Grant could feel himself getting younger by the moment as the vacation plans began to solidify. Carolyn would argue that she had to wait at home in case Alisha returned, but, he'd just have to override her objections. The Whitley's were going to shake the misery off for a few days, and like it. In his family, Grant's word was law.

The Interrogation

"They've got Ahqui!" Alisha cried as she ran to catch up with them.

"They tore him from my arms!" The little Jurrah explained, frantically.

Alisha ran past the girl and streaked after the abductors with all of her strength. Rhamas overtook her, easily and hollered after the men.

"What do you think you are doing?! Let go of that animal! You have no right to take that animal!"

The men ran into the Meeting Hall with Ahqui and the door slammed and locked behind them.

Rhamas pounded the door with both fists and demanded immediate entry. Alisha had only been a few steps behind him, and had soon joined her fists and demands to his.

The Jurrahs and Agrigars followed – all of them – young and old to save Ahqui from the man hunters. In moments, the sturdy door was kicked in, and the town advanced on the men who were holding Ahqui prone upon a table top.

Ahqui appeared to be dead.

"Ah! No!" Alisha ran to Ahqui and gathered up his lifeless body. "What have you done? What have you done! May the gods strip you of your skin and wear you as hats in hell!" She spat in the hairy one's face, and gathered Ahqui close to her, calling out his name. "Ahqui? Ahqui? Tell me that you are still with me!"

"He lives." The hairy Jurrah said, wiping Alisha's spit from his face. "He was given a sleeping draft so that we could examine him more closely."

The three men were surrounded by displeased townspeople – both Agrigar and Jurrah in the small room. Yet, they kept their seats and remained both arrogant and accusatory.

Alisha fell to the floor with Ahqui and was faint with relief at the sound on his shallow breathing. Her wedding finery was the furthest thought from her mind. She held him close, and rocked him like an infant – repeating his name again and again.

Rhamas closed the gap between himself and the three man hunters slowly. He was the definition of menace – a vengeful angel come to exact his divine retribution on the unworthy. His eyes were fire and ice, thunder and lightning. In that moment, none would have been wise to set against him. The crowd backed away, happy to give him every advantage.

"You have ruined my wedding day." Rhamas hissed. "You have endangered our companion."

"And you have harbored aliens and criminals against the Jurrah Nation." This was said with resounding boredom by Shakmun, the tallest of the man-hunters, who took this opportunity to stand. "You have lied to these people, and you have hidden truths from us, the Jurrahs who were tasked to pursue a murdering human fugitive."

There was a collective intake of breath. These accusations were not new to the assembled crowd. All had been questioned along those lines, and this matter had become a blind boil on the backsides of everyone in the village.

"I have made it clear that this animal has nothing to do with your murdering human fugitive." Rhamas said.

"We thought for a while to believe your words, Rhamas. The animal's markings were darker in places, and he truly never left the girl's side."

"As I told you." Rhamas stood his ground – arms crossed in front of him.

"But, today, as we examined your animal, we found him to be darkened curiously by charcoal that was taken from the fire. Why would you try so hard to change the animal's appearance, if you did not think him guilty?"

"Guilty? Of what could that little animal be guilty? Do you suggest that this creature is a murderer? Do you find guilt in his tendency to romp through the kitchen, begging for bits of bread and meat? What are you accusing me of, exactly? Not bathing my animal with enough frequency?"

This brought tense laughter from the assemblage. Everybody's eyes on the accusers. Every one of them afraid of what might happen next.

Shakmun walked over to where Alisha was sitting with the squear and pointed at them. "You introduced this girl as a Jurrah woman, though we know now that she is human." He strolled casually around the room, staring people down. "You hid from us the fact that she followed the Agrigars through the Ghama Traya!"

Heads were lowered now. "You keep from us that this human woman appeared in the place where we last saw Brannock, and that she travels using the same magic, and carrying the same animal."

Rhamas pulled Alisha to her feet, and placed a protective arm around her shoulders. "This woman has lived among us throughout the winter without harming anyone. She has joined my people, and become my wife within the laws of the Jurrah. My wife is guilty of no crime. The animal she carries is one she has always carried. Neither one of them will fall prey to your accusations."

"We don't wish to harm her." The hairy one, said. "Only to question her further about this man we seek. We know him to be grievously wounded, and assume that he is under someone's care. As soon as she tells us where Brannock is, we will allow her and – perhaps even her precious animal – to go free."

Rhamas positioned himself in front of Alisha and Ahqui. "Free? You threaten to detain my wife on our wedding day? I am hearing your wish to go to an early grave."

"You seem confident in the support of the population of this village." Shakmun intoned. "We have spoken to many here who are not so sure about the innocence of your human wife and her animal friend."

Rhamas scanned the room to find too many heads lowered and too many eyes averted.

"My wife hides no truths from me." His voice reverberated through the room. "She knows nothing of this human that you hunt. If there is one among you who doubts my word on these matters, come forward now."

The silence screamed his truth to the rafters.

Rhamas gave the resounding quiet a chance to settle before gathering his wife and Ahqui to leave the Hall. "I will have no more of this." He said, with finality. "Let one hand touch Alisha or Ahqui, and that shall be the hand of a dead thing."

"As for the three of you." Rhamas dismissed them with the wave of his hand. "The weather is much improved. I would make the very strong suggestion that you be on your way. This village is no longer a safe place for you to shelter."

Rhamas ushered his new family through the door and out into the courtyard. "Is he truly alive?" He asked Alisha with a whisper.

"Yes." She returned. "He lives, but barely."

"We must leave this place very soon, Alisha. I feel the wind has turned against us."

"You are well-loved, Rhamas. The people are just afraid of these angry Jurrah and their threats."

"Tonight, I take the proud donkeys' prized hats. Tomorrow, we travel well out of their reach. The Elder's prophecy has set our feet on a path that lies in distant lands."

Rhamas guided Alisha and Ahqui to the cottage of Pumgrin, a kind Agrigar who had agreed to allow the couple a night to themselves as a wedding gift. The couple's possessions were few, but Rhamas was grateful to find them arranged thoughtfully throughout their 'honeymoon' cottage. Their beds, their furs, their personal items. It was here that they found refuge from the villagers who might no longer be trusted.

The smells of their ruined wedding feast wafted through cracks in the masonry and around the windows and door. Rhamas's stomach growled for it, but knew better than to give their position away and chance another encounter with the interrogators.

As though his unblinking eyes had read Rhamas's thoughts, Pumgrin pointed to a pot of stew that he had left boiling over the fire. Rhamas thanked the Agrigar, sincerely, for his kindness, and bid him goodnight as Alisha began to remove her wedding finery.

"My love," Rhamas said, as soon as they had finished

several helpings of stew. "Tonight, I take the furs to the Wise Man to arrange our travel. I will return with all haste to you."

They kissed with longing and understanding. Both knew this to be a mission fraught with danger, yet it was not to be avoided.

Alisha locked the door securely behind her new husband and moved through the cottage to watch over the sleeping Ahqui. Though the night would be very cold, she opened a window to freshen the moldy, coffin-gone-wrong smell of the little cottage.

Trippin'

Matthew and Carolyn had been watching the evening news when Grant came through the front door with an armful of roses and a huge grin on his face. They had been momentarily stunned by the unusual sight of their father and husband's smiling face, framed in roses, standing in the doorway.

"What the fu..."

"Matthew! Watch your mouth." This from Carolyn, ever the vigilant mother.

"Honey?" She said, as Grant placed the flowers in her arms. "What are these for?" Then, she smiled, in spite of herself.

She is so lovely when she smiles. I had almost forgotten.

"Before anybody says one word, let me say that I've cleared all of the decks." He turned to Matthew. "You're not expected at school for the next two weeks."

"Cool." Skink leaned back in the overstuffed armchair

and put his feet on the coffee table.

"Grant? What are you talking about? How can he miss ...?"

"And, you, the pretty one." He said, kneeling before Carolyn for all the world as though he was about to propose marriage. "Your sister is staying here – just in case ..." He didn't have to say the rest.

"So, when are you going to tell us where we are going?" Carolyn asked, with a funny, chagrined expression that he wanted to kiss.

"Hawaii!" Grant announced, digging into his suit pocket for the tickets. "Beaches, sunshine, snorkeling..."

"Babes." Matthew interjected.

Both parents threw him a look and started to laugh.

"I was sitting in my office – surrounded by cases that I couldn't bring myself to deal with, when, it occurred to me that we haven't been able to function properly for months."

Grant knew, when he said it, that a shadow was going to fall over their faces.

"Look, family." He stood up, and addressed them as though they were a jury. "Life is precious. Every second of it.

Alisha has taught us that, if nothing else. We sit and remember our time with her – every memory a jewel in our hearts. So, now, I want to store up more of those memories! I want Carolyn jewels and Matthew jewels. I want to give you a healthy handful of husband and father jewels. Besides, I need to run away from the work that I am not doing. Let's live the life that we're not living?"

Matthew fought the urge to inject some humor regarding his father's ill-chosen 'family jewels' analogy, but let the moment pass.

Grant looked, expectantly, from Carolyn to Matthew and back.

"Gotcha." Matthew threw a thumb's up

After a brief pause, Carolyn's thumb turned up as well. "Cool." She said.

Grant heaved a sigh of relief. He hadn't expected that to go as well as it had. Now, for the biggest surprise.

"Okay, guys! Get packing! We leave for the airport in three hours!"

"You've got to be kidding." Carolyn's face was incredulous.

"Big, bad lawyers don't kid!" He posed, for dramatic

effect.

Groans turned to squeals, and the race was on. Grant leaned against the stair rail watching the fun. He hadn't felt this good in a very long time. There was excitement in that house. The sounds of drawers being rifled through and closets being raided. Frantic questions flew from room to room between family members.

"Where are the suitcases, Grant?" Carolyn called out from above.

"Mom? Are my cutoffs still on your sewing machine?"

A tear surprised Grant. It was soon followed by another. He was crying. His first instinct was to wipe them away and get control of himself, but he ignored that. The tears felt right, somehow. Necessary. Maybe, just this once, it was okay to let the big, bad lawyer cry. And, he did.

Five dozen roses lay – deserted – on the family room carpet. He had asked the florist to include every color of the rainbow, and she had complied. Grant thought they looked like a proper memorial to leave upon the grave of their grief and so he left them there.

Grant turned away and set off to pack his things. They were going to Hawaii! Yee-Haw!

"Don't worry too much about packing!" He raised his voice. "We'll just buy what we need when we get there!"

I didn't just say that, did I? Then, halfway up the stairs, he thought. *Sure I did. What the hell. The Whitley's are going to cut loose and have fun for a change.*

The First Night

Alisha sat by the window working the braids out of her hair. Ahqui was sleeping peacefully, nearby. She thought about her husband (my husband!), and the mission he had undertaken. She worried about all of the things that could go wrong, but she had great confidence in him.

Rhamas was strong, smart, fast, and bold. Some would say he had not yet reached manhood, but he was certainly well on his way. Alisha smiled, thinking about the night to come. It thrilled her to know that he would be sliding into bed beside her soon – that their kisses and stolen caresses would take them to pleasures they had never known.

The room felt hot all of a sudden, and Alisha abandoned her braids to loosen her garments and let them slip them to the floor. Now, the cool breeze could touch her body and ease the fever of her anticipation. She ran her hands over her abdomen, hips and thighs. The months of near starvation and hard work had made her tummy flat, and her muscles hard.

Alisha wished for things she couldn't have – a mirror, a razor, her Herbal Essences shampoo and cream rinse, nail clippers and polishes. So many things that would make her more beautiful for her first night.

If she had been in Maryland, there would have been a bridal shower. Alisha could imagine herself lifting sheer nighties out of brightly wrapped boxes and putting all of the bows in her hair. How different it would be to slide under furs with no clothes on, all hairy legs and armpits. Alisha grimaced.

"You hated yourself in that world." She whispered, reaching for another braid. "You thought you were too fat. You had a bad complexion, and no sense of style."

It was strange to remember her previous life in that light. Without mirrors, the Jurrah laughed and worked and made love. They didn't think about things like smooth legs and sweat-free underarms. It was easier to live this way.

Thinking that her braids had all been loosened, Alisha ran her comb through the wild waves that had been left in her hair. The comb and the cool breeze made her scalp tingle with pleasure. She wondered where Rhamas was. Could he be with the Agrigar Wise Man even now? Alisha shuddered.

"What if he refuses to take us?" She lifted her hair off

her neck to bare it to the cool breeze. "Rhamas will be called a thief, as well as a liar, and there will be no safe place for us here."

As this thought began to take root in the pit of her stomach, Alisha heard the sound of someone approaching the cottage. Her heart flew at the prospect of seeing her husband at the door, but she remained quiet – all too aware that those footsteps could belong to someone else. Someone looking for stolen pelts, perhaps.

A knock came at the door, and Alisha held her breath.

"It is your husband." She heard Rhamas, and fumbled with the latches to free the door.

At the sight of him, Alisha wrapped her arms around his body and ushered him inside, all the while showering him with kisses. "I have been so worried." She whispered into the hollow of his throat. "How did you fare with the Wise Man? Are we set to leave with him at dawn?"

Rhamas held Alisha at arm's length, taking in her nakedness, and was speechless in the face of such beauty.

Alisha smiled, shyly. She could see a growing fever in his eyes, and the sight of his reaction caused her to ache for his release.

What followed was a wordless ballet of touching, kissing, exploration and wonder. When his body covered hers in shadow, Alisha saw it above her as a shelter and a place of safety from which she would never stray. His release was a joy to her, and they fell together above the furs in a sweaty heap.

"I love you, my new husband." She whispered.

"You love a thief, then." He laughed. "For there are some who will never wear the relatives of Ahqui again."

"Yay!" She lapsed into Maryland for just a moment, but figured the meaning of her outburst would be universally understood.

"We will leave at dawn. The Wise Man was happy to come by the three pelts, and promised to conceal us from the Jurrah."

"Will he take us to Maryland?" Alisha sat up with a sudden rush of adrenaline coursing through her veins.

"He admits that he is unsure of the place called 'Maryland'." Rhamas said. "But, he tells me that he will take us to the Earth world."

"Wow." English again. "Home. I'm psyched!"

Rhamas knitted his ample brows and looked at her with consternation. "What is this you say, Alisha? This word is good?"

She laughed, and mounted him, playfully. "I guess it is my turn to be the teacher of foreign languages."

Rhamas pulled her to him and they lost all thoughts of the challenges that awaited them with the rising of the sun.

A New World

They stepped off of the plane and into a new world of palm trees and tropical breezes. Carolyn felt truly happy for the first time since...

"I'm not going to finish that thought." She kept her smile firmly in place.

"Feel that sun!" Carolyn said aloud. "Maybe we should just move here and never go home. What do you say, Matt?"

"This rocks! When do we eat?"

Grant laughed at the exchange and steered everyone towards baggage claim. "Let's get to the hotel and unpack, first, okay? We're staying 4-star this time, so I'm sure there will be a swanky restaurant within a short walk of our suite. Think you can hang on 'til then?"

Carolyn sucked in her breath and said, "Ooooh! 4-star! You've pulled out all the stops!" She was able to cut her comments short of saying *"What did we do to deserve all of this?"* It was going to be difficult to keep up the facade for two whole weeks. They needed this trip. It was just going to take some practice – saying the right things – avoiding the wrong ones.

Being at home had been hard. Carolyn had found herself constantly looking out the front windows, as though Alisha might appear at any moment. Her cell phone was never without a full charge, and she would catch herself checking it compulsively for missed calls or messages. Alisha's new winter coat still hung in the closet with the tags attached. Her hair brush, tooth brush, cosmetics, had cluttered the hall bathroom for weeks before Matt had gathered them up in a baggie and dropped them in the cabinet under the sink.

The kids had always had an awful habit of parking their backpacks and school stuff just inside the front door. Alicia's backpack had been taken by the police for examination, along with her diaries and sketch book. Upon their return, months later, Carolyn had been tempted to leave the book bag by the door, as though Alisha was just home from school and on her way to the kitchen to rummage for snacks. Ultimately, Grant had taken the whole lot into Alisha's room and shut the door.

"Here's our room. Honey, have you got the key card?"

Carolyn started at the sound of Grant's voice and produced the card from one of the outer pockets of her purse.

"Are you okay?" He asked, taking the key.

"Sure. I was just trying to remember what I packed to wear to dinner."

"Seems pretty casual here. Tomorrow we can go shopping for one of those sexy sarong things and a big flower to put behind your ear." He gave her his dopiest smile – the one she hadn't seen since...

"Don't think I won't take you up on it, either!" She teased, as the men struggled into the room with their luggage. "Wow!"

"Kawabunga! I could get used to this." Matt abandoned his bag in the doorway and headed for the balcony to check out the view.

The suite of rooms was decorated tastefully in an exotic, island theme. There were two bedrooms on opposite sides of a living room/dining room/kitchenette, with a long balcony that could be accessed by all three areas. As soon as Matthew had pulled open the french doors to the balcony, an intoxicating breeze caused the curtains to billow lazily – bringing the whole setting to life.

Carolyn felt Grant's hands slip around her waist from behind. He kissed her hair, then her neck, and whispered, "We're here, Honey. We're really here!"

She turned to kiss him, and was surprised by the passion of his response. With his arms gone to iron and his arousal pressed against her, Carolyn's heartbreak fell away like opened shackles. Their kiss was long and deep.

"Gross. You guys could take the fun out of a circus. Gack." Matthew stood, framed by the french doors, wearing a pained expression.

Everybody laughed.

The next day, Grant had made good on his promise to shop until dropping. Carolyn had been pleasantly surprised to find that she had lost several dress sizes since...

Well, anyway, her new swimsuit was a one-piece – but, it squeezed her into the shape of a woman like nothing else could. The suit was bright with large tropical blooms and palm fronds, and she had purchased a matching sarong to tie at her waist, or shoulder, depending on her mood. When they stepped out onto the beach, she could feel her husband's eyes on her body in a way that hadn't happened since before the kids were born.

Carolyn felt younger and more alive in Hawaii. She flirted with Grant, and swung her hips a bit when she walked. Her hair had grown long, and she loved to twist it up and pin it in elegant twists. From a towel on the beach, she watched her husband and son at their hilarious attempts to stand up on a surfboard. Their efforts had not only been entertaining for her, but for anyone else who came upon them. Carolyn noticed that they were taking full breaths, and moving their bodies in exuberant ways. This was life as it should be. Alisha would have wanted them to live like this.

Carolyn realized that she had just referred to her daughter in the past tense. She had tears on her face, but they were the healing kind. Life would never be the same without Alisha, but life would go on.

The Ghama Traya

The morning came too soon. Rhamas tugged his wife to wakefulness, and bid her pack their possessions as tightly as she could. They ate bread and cheese and drank water from a pitcher that Pumgrin had provided for them the night before.

They needed to be gone before the village awoke, and the village awoke plenty early. Before they left the little cottage, Rhamas drew Alisha to him for a kiss, and continued to hold her tightly. Ahqui was awake and climbing everything to explore the strange surroundings. He had never entered an Agrigar cottage – with the exception of the estate of the Wise Man – for the Agrigars considered him both dirty and possibly dangerous.

It was still dark and quite chilly when they left the village gates for the Ghama Traya. Most of the snow had melted into a muddy slush that made their tracks too easy to follow. Rhamas urged the group onward, and declined to take the time to cover their tracks.

"Where we are going," he reasoned, "none can follow."

Alisha got that roller coaster feeling in her stomach at his words. With luck, she would be home within the hour. Home! The fear of pursuit kept her enthusiasm at bay, however, and she hurried on, holding Ahqui to her breast with both arms. She knew that the squear's calm good spirits were due to the fact that walking to the Ghama Traya was a trip they had often undertaken in the past, and that he looked forward to rolling about in the snow and acting silly.

"Do you see him?" Alisha asked, as they topped the rise. "Is he there, Rhamas?"

"No." He answered, putting an arm across her back and squeezing her shoulder, encouragingly. "But we are still too far away."

"What if?"

Rhamas stopped her. "Worry not about such things. The man would refuse to show under penalty of death-by-Rhamas. This would be a very bad thing for him." He chuckled.

Alisha knew that she should trust in her husband to have made the arrangements, but she also remembered the evil gaze of the Wise Man as he demanded the fur of Ahqui. That was a creature who had built his life around deception and greed. He could have just as easily gone to the Jurrah huntsmen with a tale of theft and escape. They could all be waiting at the Ghama Traya in ambush.

Alisha stopped, abruptly, causing Rhamas to turn back and fix her with a questioning look. "Rhamas? I think we should send Ahqui ahead to scout out the Ghama Traya and see who awaits us there. He is small, and could stay out of sight much better than the two of us."

Rhamas took a moment to consider her plan and consented. "Can you instruct him to stay out of sight? There are none with whom he would be safe at this time."

Alisha nodded and knelt down to instruct the squear. "Ahqui? Sneaky, sneaky. Go to the red rock and see who is waiting there. Do not go close, Ahqui. Sneaky, sneaky, quiet, quiet. Can you see and come back? Bad, Bad Jurrah might be there. We must hide from Bad Bad Jurrah."

Ahqui nodded, gravely, and padded off into the snow and slush. Alisha was proud to see the way in which he hugged the earth and moved with stealth. Alisha and Rhamas waited behind – scarcely breathing – watching nervously for Ahqui's safe return. It was many tense moments before they saw the squear speeding towards them with an expression of alarm clear upon his features. Covered with sludge and wet, he leapt into Alisha's arms and shivered there.

"Tell us, Ahqui. Were the Bad Jurrah there?"

Ahqui turned his eyes to hers and nodded a clear "Yes!"

Alisha took in a breath and sought Rhamas for a plan. His first utterance was a Jurrah phrase meaning 'dung of a Garron whore.'

"We must hide ourselves. We must do this quickly, for they will soon realize that we are late."

The couple looked around them seeing nothing remotely resembling a place of hiding. The village would no longer harbor them, the forest lay past the Ghama Traya where they would have to cross a large expanse of open field. They were trapped.

Ahqui begged and squirmed to be set down. He would not listen to Alisha's warnings, and he would no longer submit to her embrace. Unable to endure his thrashings, she finally did as he demanded and set him down upon the ground at her feet. Within seconds, he was running a course that took him behind the Ghama Traya and into an area of drifted snow. Once there, he looked for them to follow – bobbing up and down frantically until they ducked down and started in his direction.

The little squear began to dig. Alisha had never seen him dig. He was a machine! Ahqui burrowed deeply into the drift and urged them to do the same.

"I believe you have a very smart friend in Ahqui." Rhamas said. "He is building us a place to hide."

Alisha looked on, wide-eyed. "There?" She asked incredulous.

"Is there a better place?" Rhamas answered, adding his efforts to the squear's to make room for the three of them.

It was in this way that Alisha, Rhamas, and Ahqui outsmarted the Wise Man of Agrigar and the Bad, Bad Jurrah huntsmen. As a bonus, of sorts, they had been able to hear the screams and cries of the Wise Man as he was being beaten for failing to produce their quarry. The Jurrahs accused the Wise Man of leading them away from the village to allow the fugitives to escape, unseen, in another direction!

"You have used the Ghama Traya, Alisha?" Rhamas whispered.

"Yes. It brought me here from Natalo II."

"You will have to use it again, my wife." He said. "We must be away from this place in a hurry. There is no other path left to us."

Even as Alisha objected in her heart, she knew that Rhamas was right. They must travel to another world in order to be safe from those who pursued them. "But, I don't know how." She said, in a whisper.

"We will place our hands on it together and hope we land safely in another place."

Alisha nodded. Ahqui's bowels loosened in a growing pool that soon encompassed the couple's boots.

"He does that when he's scared." Alisha explained, trying not to breathe through her nose.

"So do I." Answered Rhamas. "But, I am not afraid. My wife is a traveler from another world, and she will take us safely from this place."

"Sure." Alisha intoned. "World traveler. Other place. Safe. All of that."

Touching the Stone

The three of them waited in silence, long after the sounds of the huntsmen had moved out of range. They knew that hours were passing, but had already decided to risk using the Ghama Traya as soon as they reached it to avoid capture.

"I think they have gone." Rhamas stated. His face was still screwed up in response to the smell of Ahqui's feces and urine.

"Are you ready? We're going to have to make a run for it. I think I am going to use the part of the stone that will take us to Natalo II, first. That will give me more time to consider our next move."

Ahqui, sensing that the group was gathering up for a move, climbed into Alisha's arms, smearing her with excrement on the way up.

"I don't think that is our best move." Argued Rhamas. "The Wise Man will look there first."

"Do you think the hunters will follow him through the

Ghama Traya? I thought Jurrah avoided such travel?"

Rhamas crouched at the entrance to their hideout and thought. "What if he sends Agrigars in after us?"

"Agrigars? Do you think any of them would follow him with that mission in mind? You are well-loved among them, and I..."

"You make good talk." Rhamas dropped his head into his hands. "Are you afraid to travel to a new place?"

Alisha paused. "Absolutely."

"This is not a time for being afraid, my wife." He ducked out of the smelly depression that they had dug into the snow bank and stood to look about. Soon, Alisha saw his face framed by the entrance. "It is clear now. It is time."

Alisha pushed their rolled up possessions out of the snow bank and followed shortly after – still cradling Ahqui in her arms. She had been sitting for so long, that Rhamas had to help her to a standing position. The fresh air was invigorating, and a relief from the closed space where they had spent the last three hours. She brushed the snow from her pants with a free hand.

"Okay, Husband." Alisha smiled, mischievously. "Let's go find a safe dimension where you can make arrangements for our dinner. I'm starving." Without warning, the thought of her mother's chicken and dumplings popped into her mind. Was it possible that they could end up back home? Alisha could feel a change in her pulse as they raced together towards the red rock.

The rock had been abandoned, and they went to it with a certain reverence. Rhamas kept a nervous watch as Alisha circled the Ghama Traya deciding which part to touch.

This decision is life or death. Where will it take us? How will I know?

Alisha bit her lip and concentrated.

If I came upon this rock while walking through the corn maze, where would I have touched it?

But, Alisha didn't recall having seen a rock in the corn maze, much less having touched one. There wasn't any way of knowing…

"Rhamas." Alisha commanded, making up her mind at last. "Come here to me. I don't know how this works, so you must hold us both, tightly, lest we become separated."

He slipped his arms around her waist and pressed himself against her body in a most seductive way. Alisha smiled, in spite of her nerves.

"Okay, everybody. Look at the point where I am placing my hand, and try to remember it, as that is likely to be the best way to return."

Ahqui wrapped his arms around Alisha's neck and squeezed tightly. His unhappiness at having to endure such a journey again, most evident.

Then, as they all held their breath, Alisha's hand reached out and pressed – full-palmed – against the chosen surface of the Ghama Traya.

There was an instant change of temperature to the atmosphere, and there were sounds…

Where the Fuck are We Now?

Where the fuck are we now?

The words had come to Alisha's mind before her eyes had even had a chance to open. She didn't let them out of her mouth this time, though neither Rhamas nor Ahqui would have known enough English to be offended by them.

"Did it work?" Alisha asked, with her eyelids clamped firmly together.

Rhamas did not reply soon enough, and she was about give way to terror, when he said, "Yes. We are nowhere I have ever known."

"Is that a good thing, or a bad thing?" She asked, still refusing to look.

Alisha could feel Ahqui's grasp on her loosen, she allowed him to slide to the ground at her feet.

Rhamas touched her face, lightly, and kissed her mouth. "Open your eyes, my love." He whispered. "We are wherever we are. It is time to find out where that is."

Alisha was truly afraid. Her biggest fear was that she would open her eyes and not be home. Slowly, however, and at her husband's urging, she had allowed them to open.

The first thing that Alisha saw was the ravaged cornfield. It had been much the same as the one they had just left behind, but the air in this place was warmer, and the earth was dry and hard rather than muddy with melted snow.

A new sound caused Alisha to whirl to her left, and there, at the edge of the field, was a road. She gulped down tears as she followed the black car with her eyes.

"How does that move?" Rhamas asked. "There are no oxen."

"I don't know." Alisha answered. And, she didn't – as the egg-shaped car had been hovering two feet above a road paved with blue glass. "Rhamas." She turned her tear-filled eyes on him. "This is not my home. I don't know where we are."

"We are in a good place, my love. Any place is good where there are no Jurrah huntsmen lying in wait."

"Ahqui!" Alisha called. "Get back here!" Her hand came up to shade her eyes from the sun.

The little squear had been turning forward somersaults

across the field and had gotten further away from her than she had thought prudent.

Ahqui's face popped up as he stood, and his mouth was open with a questioning look.

"Come here, Ahqui." Alisha said, more gently this time. "We are in a strange place. We should stay together."

"Let's find water, Rhamas. One or two of us could use a bath." Alisha looked down at her soiled pants and boots.

"Yes. I am thirsty, as well. In which direction do you suggest we look?" Rhamas, for once, seemed very out of his element.

"Ahqui?" Alisha kneeled down to the returned squear. "Water?"

Ahqui's little black nose worked furiously as he revolved a complete 360 degrees, trying to catch a scent. It wasn't long until he stood back up and pointed with certainty towards a cluster of trees in the distance. Alisha and Rhamas exchanged glances, as they could see no river running through the clearing, but simply picked up their belongings and consented to follow behind. After all, the squear was a woodland animal, and had a better nose for such things.

The walk had been a short one, and the party had soon

found themselves in a shady glen standing before a clear glass pedestal, covered by a matching glass dome. Ever the adventurer, Alisha stepped forward and lifted the dome by its handle. Underneath the lid she had discovered a basin that was full to the rim with clear, fresh water. As each explorer bent to drink from it, the bowl refilled – as if by magic.

Alisha had examined it closely for any sign of plumbing, or opening, or spout from which the fresh water could enter and the soiled water could drain – but had found no evidence of either and shrugged her shoulders.

"It's good." She said. "I don't know how it works, but it is fresh and cold."

"Ah." Rhamas wiped the water from his mouth with the back of one hand. "You see? A good place."

Rhamas pulled a leather flask from their bundle of possessions and filled it with the delicious water. He then began to remove his clothing as if to bathe.

Alisha watched him undress with a wry smile on her face. Rhamas was very handsome and his body had been toned by many years of hunting and building and being a proud male of the Jurrah tribe.

"Here." She rifled through the pack and offered him the

remains of her ragged tee shirt.

This, Rhamas dipped into the basin many times to wipe himself clean as his new wife watched with amusement. His muscles rippled under the wet rag, and his manhood thickened at her unflinching appraisal. Alisha was surprised to see his cheeks flush with embarrassment. Rhamas chose this moment to turn his attention towards Ahqui.

"Now, it is your turn!" Rhamas said, chasing after and scooping up the stinky squear. However, Ahqui wasn't about to let himself be bathed by any Jurrah, and he fought a winning battle – being dunked and scrubbed instead by Alisha until he sat, dripping and somewhat resentful, at the base of a young Elm.

Alisha approached Rhamas with a coy expression, and relieved him of the wash cloth without getting close enough to touch his naked body. Rhamas, for his part, settled onto the grass to watch Alisha remove her soiled tunic and pants, revealing her young breasts and taut belly. Shyly, she turned away as she began to wash herself, giving her new husband a glorious view of her smooth, white buttocks.

"Es Chumi lat bantas muc!" He teased in Jurrah -- the English equivalent of "I think you've missed a spot."

Again and again, the magic basin filled. The water had never clouded with their filth that it hadn't instantly re-freshened Alisha had thought this to be a thing wrought by sorcery, rather than machination, and she said as much.

"For this time, let us just be thankful that it exists." Rhamas observed. "I am seeing that there are many things to learn in this *paclusin*." (The Jurrah word for 'heaven').

"This is not a heaven, husband." Alisha wondered how she would explain alternative realities, dimensions, and worlds – realized that she was out of her depth on the subject and let it go.

"Where else could carts fly and water fill a bowl from the air?" Rhamas argued, good-naturedly. "You can name it what you will; to me, it will be one of the ten heavens of Mantaroon."

They ate a modest meal of bread and cheese from their rations. Their clothing was cleaned and allowed to dry as they rested, peacefully, within the small cluster of trees. The troupe had so exhausted themselves in their efforts to escape Natalo I, that they had allowed the distant sounds of vehicles whirring by and the chirping of crickets to lull them to sleep.

Later, they awoke to darkness, four moons, and a million bright stars shining down upon them.

"Rhamas?"

"Yes, my wife."

"You were right. This must be one of the ten heavens of Montaroon. I don't know what I was thinking."

Rhamas smiled and his white teeth lit the night all the more for their brilliance. "I forgive you, of course. You have not yet learned to trust in my great wisdom and knowledge of all things."

"Bullshit." Alisha replied, rolling onto her stomach and propping her head upon her hands. She laughed at his confused expression.

"What is this 'bullshit' that you speak to me? Does it have meaning I should know?"

Alisha thought about that for a minute. "It is an endearment that my people use when they feel another's words are especially meaningful."

"Ah." Rhamas's smile widened. "Prepare yourself to be using this Maryland word a great deal."

Alisha moved to kiss Rhamas before she lost her grip on the laughter that was building in her chest.

"Consider me prepared." She said.

The Paclusin of Montaroon

With their water skins filled, and wearing relatively clean clothing and boots, the group decided to gather up their possessions and follow alongside the strange road in the hopes that it would lead them to a village (or – as Alisha hoped) a grocery store or hamburger joint.

Alisha talked about the see-through road using words like "glass" and "polymer," being herself unsure of the material that had been used to compose it. She talked about "magnetic strips," and "cars" that had been fitted with "magnets" of different "polarities" to help them move forward and float above the road at the same time. Rhamas walked beside her with his mind working hard to keep up.

My wife knows of many things. He thought. *Maryland is having many wondrous ideas of which I have no knowledge, and this makes me as a child in her eyes.*

"I'll bet that they use some kind of electro-magnetic gadgetry to purify the water, too." Alisha said. She shrugged and shook her head. "I don't know how they do it. I've never seen anything like that before."

I am not remembering all of the words she is saying! Rhamas raked both hands through his hair with frustration. *This is too much for learning in one day. She must soon be silent, or my head will break open with too many of her Maryland words!*

Alisha noticed her husband's silence and growing frustration, though she had no idea as to the cause of it. She allowed Ahqui to run along beside them so as to relieve the aching of her arms and to take Rhamas's hand in hers as they continued on their journey.

Before long, the fields gave way to – what looked to Alisha like – small homesteads and storage buildings. Rhamas had wanted to approach these, but Alisha had strongly opposed the idea for a couple of reasons: Firstly, she had never seen brightly-colored-glass-domed homesteads; and further, she had no idea what kinds of beings made their homes in brightly-colored-glass-domed homesteads.

As they walked, Alisha and Rhamas saw many large blue and yellow glass domes dotting the countryside, with the occasional – smaller, but no less beautiful – red domes occurring less frequently.

The afternoon sun glittered too brightly from the road and the dwellings, and it wasn't long before Alisha was fighting off a migraine. As we established earlier, Alisha was in the habit of shutting herself into her bedroom with two Excedrin Migraine tablets and a glass of water when suffering a headache of this severity. Now, in one of the ten heavens of Montaroon, she found herself without any such resources. Her face paled, and her eyes squinted shut. All conversation stopped, and Rhamas and Ahqui exchanged worried glances.

"My Alisha?" Rhamas inquired. "You are not well?"

"No."

"Shall we stop to rest and drink water?"

"No."

Ahqui shook his head knowingly at Rhamas and clamped his furry hand over his own mouth to encourage a time of silence.

Rhamas took the suggestion seriously, and the three traveled on without speaking.

The road made for smoother walking, and had remained unnaturally cool throughout the hottest part of the day, so the troupe walked side-by-side along its glistening surface. The blue-glass road had a dark substance inserted just under the surface of the center line. Rhamas wondered if the strip was one of the magnets that Alisha had spoken of.

"There are no birds in this paclusin." Rhamas noted, as they walked. "This is something strange to me."

Alisha shielded her eyes and scanned the brilliant blue skies at considerable cost to her throbbing eye sockets.

"If it is, in fact, a paclusin." She muttered, snarkily. Then, in a more conciliatory tone, said: "There were none in – she hesitated only a moment to substitute the locally-preferred name – Natalo II, either."

Several times along the way, the blue-glass road was met by roads of other colors. A yellow-glass road crossed East and West, making for a bright green intersection. Alisha had noticed a complete absence of road signs, and had come to the conclusion that the color of each route must give information enough. Her head pounded, and the light glinting from so many glassy surfaces was threatening to burst her skull into splinters.

They had been going like this for many miles without seeing one magic cart, and Rhamas began to wonder what they would do if they ... well ... did?

"Alisha, darling one?" Rhamas asked in a near whisper. "What will we do if one of the flying carts approaches us?"

There was a long pause.

"I would strongly suggest that we move out of its way," came the terse reply.

Rhamas and Ahqui exchanged glances again. Rhamas nodded, raising his eyebrows and shrugging his shoulders at the squear. The group journeyed quietly onward.

Finally, in the early evening, Alisha stepped from the road and moved towards an outcropping of rock under a hillside. Ahqui slid to the grassy lawn and stretched and rolled and yawned widely before dropping to all fours and running towards the cool and shady spill of boulders Alisha was striding towards.

Rhamas offered Alisha a flask, from which she drank greedily. Then he gave Ahqui a generous mouthful before pouring great gulps of the crystalline water down his own throat.

"We will stop here for the night." Alisha declared, wiping water from her lips and leaving a dusty smear across her face.

"It is a good place." Rhamas agreed. "It will shelter us from anyone approaching on the road, and will protect us from two sides if there is an attack." He pointed to the way the rocks had cut into the hillside at an angle. The shadows will conceal us, as well."

Alisha and Rhamas unrolled their bedding and pulled some bread and cheese from a pouch for their dinner. This was divided three ways and consumed in silence, as it was the last of their food and there was no certainty when (or if) the next meal would become available.

Rhamas watched as Alisha rubbed at her temples and winced in pain.

"You have the pain in your head?" He asked. "I know the cure for this."

Alisha opened one eye and looked at Rhamas. "You do?"

"You must wait here." He said, standing. "I will try to find some of the ingredients further up the hill. It will also be a good way to see what lies ahead."

"Yep. I will wait right here." She half-moaned. "Just try to move me." Alisha sank to her furs and rolled her pack into a pillow. Carefully, she curled onto her side and lowered her head to its less-than-comfy bulk.

"Ouch." She moaned, quietly. "Ouch, ouch, ouch."

Ahqui took up a position behind her head and got to

work, diligently checking for parasites.

"Ah. That feels good." Alisha mumbled to the squear – after which, she closed her eyes and allowed herself to sleep.

The Hills Are Alive

As the moons and the stars rose to take their turn in the night sky, Rhamas explored the forested hillside. He stopped often to search out the herbs and roots that he knew would ease Alisha's pain. The nascilian ferns grew only in the shadows of great trees, and their roots could be mashed into a creamy substance that – when combined with other ingredients – had been used by his people for generations to relieve pain.

He knelt to gather all that he found, and tucked each prize into a small leather pouch that he carried at his belt. The night was growing cool, and a breeze lifted the hair off of his brow in such a pleasing way that Rhamas pulled his hair from his face and held it off of his neck, inviting the gentle gusts to dry and cool the sweat of a long day.

This paclusin was a beautiful place that was set aside for the most righteous of spirits. Rhamas knew that he was blessed among men to have taken Alisha as his wife, as without her, he might never have been permitted to cross into this land while yet alive. Muanti had uttered his blessing upon them, saying, "The doors of countless worlds will swing open before you."

Rhamas bowed his head as a thought that he had been pushing away for days settled upon his shoulders like a heavy cloak.

What if Alisha grows tired of my ignorance? She knew of 'glass,' before coming upon the bright roads, she had spoken lightly of it, dismissing my awe as one would a child.

While Alisha had been with his people, she had appeared as one of them. The Jurrah ways had come easily to her, and she had seemed happy. With his tribe around him, Rhamas had been able to stand as a man – knowledgeable in the skills of hunting and providing for a woman and children. But that world was behind them now. What if he no longer knew enough to be a good husband to her?

She says this word, 'bullshit.' to me, and she thinks me too stupid to guess at its meaning. I laugh with her, and I see the love in her face, but I fear this word. This talk means that she thinks of me as an infant – ignorant of the things she knew all along without telling.

Rhamas felt a tightening in his chest, and he could not discern whether it was sadness that gripped him, or dread. He closed the pouch at his waist and continued up the hill to its summit to view the road ahead. His breath caught in his throat at the vista that lay below. It was light as he'd never seen it, glowing from multicolored domes that bloomed like flowers in the night. So many domes. So many colors. The roads which threaded in and among the dwellings were also alight, with magic carts – like droplets – sliding along their lengths to add a hypnotic aspect of movement to the unfolding kaleidoscope below.

Rhamas fell to his knees and stared at the beauty of this until his eyes watered. As a child, he had heard every story about the paclusins of Montaroon, but no Jurrah would have been equal to the telling of such a tale as this. This light was not made of fire. It was a smokeless, chimney-less village. Could God's finger have touched each dwelling as he had the stars above?

I will not speak of this light to Alisha. I will not stand in wonderment of it, but will take it as a known thing – without question. There is much to learn, but I do not have to play the idiot each time a new miracle makes itself known to me.

Rhamas gazed until eyes were tired, and his body ached. If Alisha agreed to venture into the glass village in the morning, there would be much need of his vigilance. He should return and get some sleep.

How does a man sleep who travels through heaven? He asked himself.

Rhamas returned to their campsite via a different route, in order to widen his search for plants and herbs useful in the creation of many remedies and salves. Suddenly, from a thicket of brambles, there came a sound and some movement that caught his attention. There, from a kneeling position, Rhamas pulled a slingshot from his belt and armed it silently with a stone that lay at his feet.

En snelbista tans echosti! He thought, joyously, as he watched the tan and white striped creature hop out of the undergrowth and into his line of sight. Smat! Rhamas grabbed the stunned animal adroitly and slit its throat with his knife.

"You will make a fine breakfast for us!" He beamed, proudly. "I will go to my wife bearing gifts, as a husband should!"

But, as Rhamas prepared the carcass, tiny rustlings came to his ears from the thicket. His smile faded.

She had little ones. This thought saddened him. *They will not live without their mother.*

Rhamas knew that he would have to round up the bunnies and slaughter them, too. To let them starve or suffer would be unnecessarily cruel. The tiny kits would not yield much meat, but would *"thicken a stew more than pebbles"* (his father's words), so Rhamas dispatched the litter of five humanely, and prepared their carcasses as best he could.

He reached the campsite long after sunset to find Alisha and Ahqui asleep – Alisha's gentle snores bringing a smile to his lips. Rhamas wasted no time in joining them, and there he slept without dreaming.

Death at Dawn

Ahqui had been first to awaken the next morning. Finding himself unsupervised, the squear had tumbled away from the campsite to find a tree to climb or a shrubbery to rustle about in. By the time Rhamas and Alisha had risen, however, and stretched their cramped bodies into alertness, Ahqui was nowhere to be found.

"Ahqui!" Alisha had called, concern etched on her face.

"Do you feel better this morning, my wife?" Rhamas scanned her features for signs of the pain she had carried the day before.

"Ahqui is gone!" She answered, instead. "We must find him!"

"Let us prepare breakfast." Rhamas quipped. "He has never missed a meal in my knowing of him."

"Rhamas! I am afraid! Please, we must find him!"

And, so, the couple split up to search for the squear, calling his name over and over through the surrounding countryside with no response. Two hours later, with nothing to show for their efforts, Alisha and Rhamas met again at the campsite with fear in their hearts.

Alisha dropped her head into her hands and cried – her hair falling loosely around her face like a curtain. Rhamas tried to comfort her, but knew that neither of them would have peace until they had Ahqui safe within their possession once more.

"He would not leave me." Alisha sobbed. "I know he wouldn't."

"Perhaps he is playing in the woods and has forgotten himself for a time." Rhamas ventured. "He can find us whenever he wishes, my love, he has only to sniff us out." At that, he lifted an arm and made as if to smell his armpit before screwing up his face to mimic Ahqui's dismay at his pungent aroma.

She smiled a little, but the tears continued to run down her cheeks.

"He comes to me when I call him." Alisha moaned. "He always comes to me."

Rhamas wrapped Alisha into his embrace and rocked her as he would a frightened child. "Shh." He smoothed her hair away from her face and did his best to soothe her. "He will be well. You will see. Come, let us prepare a meal and later, when we are strengthened, we will search again."

"We ate the last of it, yesterday." Alisha sniffed. "There is nothing."

Rhamas lifted her face to smile into her eyes. "Aha. But, your good husband, who does love you more than life, did hunt through the night and bring you a fat snelbista for your breakfast!"

Through her tears, Alisha smiled at him, and Rhamas felt his heart grow in his chest.

"Come! See this bounty your husband has provided!" He proudly unrolled the packet of meat for Alisha and regretted it, instantly, as her expression was one of horror at the sight of the tiny bodies that lay alongside the robust carcass of the mother *snelbista.*

"What have you done?" Alisha's voice was accusatory. "You have slaughtered a mother and her kits? What point was there in bringing their tiny bodies to me in this way?"

Rhamas was hurt by the look she bestowed upon him, and he wanted to explain his actions – at first – but his injured pride gave way to anger before the words could arrange themselves into sentences, and Rhamas stalked away to build a fire so that he could begin preparation of the stew.

"How could you have done something so cruel?" Alisha called after him. "And you lay their shortened lives before me as a gift? For this, I am supposed to be grateful?"

Rhamas trembled with emotion as he went about his task. Just a few hours ago, he had been sure that they were guests in a miraculous heaven! Alisha had been sleeping with her face buried in Ahqui's ruff. All had been peace and tranquility. His memory took him back to the grueling ordeal it had been to gather the little creatures and break their necks – one at a time – as the hot tears had threatened to overspill his lashes.

The lessons learned at his father's side had been hard ones, but it was those very skills for which he had been most grateful. He had only done as was best. Alisha would have to be made to see the wisdom of his decisions.

A Jurrah woman would not have dared to question her husband in such a way. He thought. *A Jurrah woman would have been proud of him for making sure the little ones did not suffer.*

Rhamas poured the remaining water into a pot and set it to simmer on the fire. Still seething with countless emotions, he added meat and herbs to the pot, and stirred it more vigorously than was absolutely necessary.

What of Ahqui? Where could he have gone? Alisha will perish of a broken heart if he is not found. Could he have fallen prey to a mountain lion, or wolf? Perhaps he was injured by a hunter's snare and is suffering a slow and agonizing death? He winced.

It was as Rhamas settled into this latest set of worries, that Alisha had approached in silence and laid a hand upon his shoulder.

Rhamas turned his head to look at her.

"I am sorry, husband." Alisha spoke gently. "The stew smells delicious, and my hunger teaches me the value of your gift."

His relief was instant and complete. Rhamas pulled her to him and whispered fervently into her hair. "The little ones would have suffered..." He started, to explain, but Alisha put a finger to his lips.

"Of course, husband. Forgive me my ignorance. My heart was troubled."

"As was my own." He kissed her forehead and cheek and mouth.

So caught up in reconciliation were they, that the urgent tugs and whimperings of a muddy and starving Ahqui had, at first, gone unnoticed.

"Ahqui!" They both exclaimed in unison.

"And, didn't I tell my wife that a certain poorly-behaved animal was not likely to forgo a meal?"

The laughter that ensued was more healing than any herbal tea ever brewed, and what wasn't healed by the laughter was sated by the feast that followed it.

The First Jurrah

Alisha filled her stomach with the rabbit stew, and treated herself to an extra helping. Rhamas had combined the meat with exotic root vegetables, and seasoned it with delicate herbs so that the taste and aroma were irresistible. The joy at having Ahqui back at her side had given Alisha a sharp appetite and a more hopeful outlook than she had enjoyed in days.

Rhamas had reclined across from her, and was artfully presenting his latest narrative entitled, *"Blooms of Light in the City of Heaven."* This telling would be the first ever told by a Jurrah, but would not be the last. Long after Rhamas was gone, the Jurrah people would gather to hear a story they called: *"Blooms of Light in the City of Heaven as seen by Rhamas, The Traveler of Worlds."*

As they had wasted much of the morning searching, arguing and cooking, the troupe had declared the remainder of the day as a time of rest and planning. Alisha listened to Rhamas with a face full of wonderment as he wove his words into a glorious tapestry of color and light.

"And, the roads lit up, too?" Alisha asked, breathless.

"That they did, my wife!" Rhamas swelled with pride. "And, from the hilltop, I saw the magic carts flying about – starting and stopping. The sight was near enough to the beauty of your own face that I could have fainted away and rolled down the hillside only to die alone among the meadow's waving grasses."

Alisha lowered her lashes and smiled at the compliment. What followed was a contented silence. As she reclined by Rhamas's side, Alisha watched a tiny black lizard – a skink – as it climbed out from between some rocks to warm himself in the sun.

"Skink," she whispered.

"You speak?" Rhamas asked, following her gaze.

"My brother," her head bowed.

Rhamas saw the lizard, but misunderstood the reference. "The black lizard? This is your brother?"

Alisha smiled. "No, of course, not." She met his eyes. "My brother has the friend-name 'Skink,' which is what my people call the lizard."

"Then, I feel most sorry towards your brother." Rhamas commiserated.

Alisha busied herself picking up the plates and scouring out the cooking pot with a handful of sand. Rhamas could sense the longing in her, and also the sadness of that memory.

"You wish very much to go home?" He said, gently.

"I do."

"Is it your wish to return to the Ghama Traya and try again, rather than travel onward to the Domed City?"

"Sometimes," she said, reflectively. "Yet, I am curious about what lies ahead in this world. Your words have drawn beautiful images behind my eyes." Her mouth turned slightly up on one corner and she fluttered her eyelashes, playfully.

"We have much life ahead of us to travel these worlds." He said. "If it is your wish, we can search into many realities until we find the one you seek. There is nothing but curiosity keeping us here."

"I worry that the beauty will hold great danger for us, Rhamas." She confessed.

"The three of us? I am sure that there is nothing on heaven or earth that would dare to harm such an imposing gathering of wit and brawn!" Rhamas grabbed Alisha around the waist and danced her about like a bride.

"Why, this beast, alone, would strike fear into the heart

of a giant!"

The couple observed Ahqui, as he lay on his back in the grass, legs waving in the air as he rubbed his overstuffed tummy. Their laughter caught his attention, and he rolled to his feet and waddled over to them as if to say, "What's funny, now? What have I missed?"

The squear stood, stretching his hands up to Alisha so that he might be picked up.

"You see that?" Rhamas joked. "A horrible beast – ready to tear an enemy into small pieces!"

Ahqui scratched his nose before returning his full attention to Alisha – arms supplicating.

After cleaning up and packing their belongings into tight bundles once again, it was decided that the group would ascend together to spend the night within view of the city as Rhamas had done. Alisha secretly hoped to catch sight of the inhabitants of that place. She had felt a certain disquiet from the moment they had arrived in this reality, and needed assurance that she was not leading the three of them into a dangerous situation.

Miraculously, Alisha's headache had not returned. Her face opened up into the approachable and unwavering flower that her companions knew and loved. Rhamas, hoping never to spend a day with the scary Alisha again, assured her that he carried everything necessary to combat the pain of any future episodes. As they hiked up the hillside, Rhamas pulled more roots and herbs and instructed Alisha on their usage and efficacies.

"This tuber," Rhamas explained, "has within it a white cream that can be used on an open wound, or taken internally when mixed into a tea or broth."

Alisha listened to her beloved husband, but not as closely as she might have. The latticed shadows from the leafy wood passed across his face and shoulders making him seem more like a figure in a fairytale than the flesh-and-blood man she had taken for her husband. His hair had grown longer in the past few weeks, and the dark waves of it tumbled past his collar and onto his shoulders where the curls might lift with the gentlest of breezes.

Rhamas must have sensed her lack of attention, for he stopped talking and took Alisha's hand, flashing her the smile that had won her heart.

"We will find your brother, the lizard." Rhamas assured her. "We will find him together, and show him how fortunate you have been to find a protector in me."

Alisha rolled her eyes at this, and they both laughed, heartily.

How long have I known this man? Alisha mused. *Only a handful of weeks and a sprinkling of days. How is it that I feel his body as an extension of my own, and that I am now grateful to God for the missteps that delivered me into his embrace?*

Rhamas witnessed Alisha's retreat into thoughtfulness and worried that he might lose her. He had taken a woman to wife who had more knowledge than he had even yet to discover. How could she help but compare him to the men of Maryland who knew of glass, and lights, and carts without oxen? He bowed his head and a shadow covered his features.

They reached the top long before nightfall, but could barely set up camp before Ahqui began to yawn and tug at his ears. He had worn himself out making everyone sick with worry that morning, apparently, and he wasted no time in finding a comfy place to settle and nap.

The Inhabitants of Heaven

Alisha cradled the sleeping squear within her arms as the sun dropped beyond the horizon. Rhamas had told no lies regarding the spectacle she was about to see, and the two of them had sat together upon the hilltop, watching the city light up into a myriad of glowing colors under a canopy of stars and moons.

"What I wouldn't give for a pair of binoculars." Alisha muttered.

Rhamas wanted to ask what she meant, but did not – deciding instead to listen and learn.

The glow of the city was lovely, but it also created halos that made tiny details impossible to decipher. While Alisha could see that cars stopped in front of domes, she was unable to make out the shapes of the inhabitants as they disembarked.

"I need to get a closer look." She said to Rhamas.

"Do you think this is wise?" He asked. "Once we reach the plain that approaches, we will be in full view."

"Yes." Alisha agreed. "But, now, we will have the darkness on our side, and the brightness of their own lights may blind them to us."

"This, you say, having never seen their eyes."

"Rhamas, I must get a closer look." Alisha argued, turning her most earnest face to his. "If they are shaped like us, then there may be a way to conceal our appearance enough to pass freely among them."

"And, if they crawl on their bellies and taste the air with forked tongues?"

"I'm being serious." She said.

"So am I."

"Rhamas," Alisha hesitated. "I approached the Agrigars because it was that, or freeze to death. They had a head and the recommended number of appendages, and gave every sign of belonging to a civilized society."

Many of her words made no sense to him, but he allowed them to pass like a stream over rocks, sifting what meaning he could from the context.

"This city is very advanced. Much more so than the one I came from. If they are like us in appearance, I believe we will have an easier time being accepted. If not, then we would be wise to ascertain whatever we can about their habits – and diet..." The pause was meaningful.

"Ah."

"Yes." Alisha confirmed. "But, there is another worry, husband. In my time, there were alarm systems." She stopped, knowing that she was leaving him behind. "There were magical traps that warned of an enemy's approach. It is possible that we could be injured or taken captive if we stumbled across one."

"Could we not send Ahqui to observe the inhabitants and check for magical traps?"

Alisha stroked the sleeping squear and looked thoughtful. "I think I could make him understand, but, he is so little."

Rhamas softened his eyes. "Yes, my love. It is his size that gives him the best advantage."

Alisha could see his point, but wasn't sure what good it would do to send Ahqui in as a scout when he would be unable to relate much of what he had seen upon his safe return.

Rhamas cleared his throat. "If we send Ahqui." He paused. "We would have more information than we do now – and we would not have put ourselves at risk."

Alisha did not answer, but continued to stroke Ahqui,

lovingly.

"We can wait until after midnight." Rhamas added. "Ahqui is an animal, Alisha. He is much less likely to be considered out of place – if he is seen at all."

"I will do this, Rhamas." She answered, in Jurrah. "We are not pressed to enter the city at all. We will learn what we can, and then decide whether to continue forward or return to the Ghama Traya."

Rhamas nodded, satisfied.

"I must have something to write on." She mumbled. "It will help us remember where each touch point on the Ghama Traya leads."

Rhamas knew the word, 'remember,' but had no understanding of what it meant 'to write.' Again, he simply nodded.

Alisha thought about the scraps of white leather left over from her wedding outfit.

Would a piece of charcoal leave a permanent mark upon the leather? She thought. *No. I am certain that it would wipe away too easily. Perhaps I could burn marks into it?*

"Let the little guy sleep." Rhamas said. "Come here to me."

The couple sat in silhouette upon the hilltop. Rhamas's arm encircling Alisha's waist. Their eyes turned towards the glorious tableau that lay before them.

Reconnaissance

Rhamas awoke to find Alisha fast asleep at his side. He grasped her shoulder, and kissed her cheek.

"Alisha." Rhamas whispered. "It is time."

Alisha sat up and rubbed at her eyes, looking about as if she wasn't sure where she was. Seeing the moons above and the lights of the city below, she came to remember their plan for Ahqui. The squear was curled up on one side and snoring.

"Are you sure this is a good idea?" She asked, clearly hesitant to disturb Ahqui.

"It is worth a try." He said.

Alisha scooped up the sleeping Ahqui as a mother would lift an infant from his crib. She fixed his head upon her shoulder and patted his back.

"Ahqui? Wake up, little guy. It is time to wake up for Alisha."

Rhamas could see Ahqui's face over Alisha's shoulder,

and had to smile as the squear forced one eye open, tried to focus on it on him, and then drowsily closed it again.

"Ahqui?" Alisha set him down on two feet and kept hold of his hands. Ahqui, now awake, but groggy, looked up at her.

"Ahqui help Alisha now?"

The squear nodded and yawned. Alisha pointed to the beautiful city and said, "Ahqui go see? Come and tell Alisha? Human? Jurrah? Like us?"

Ahqui looked towards the city and back to Alisha. He seemed confused for a moment, and then pointed at the lights and back at himself with a questioning look on his face. Alisha nodded.

"Yes. Ahqui must be sneaky."

The word "sneaky" was one that registered in the squear's mind, as it had been used often in the games that they played together. Gradually, the understanding rose in his eyes. The squear nodded, and bounded off on all fours down the hill towards the lights of the city.

"Do you think he understands you?" Rhamas asked.

"Yes."

"That is a wonderment in itself."

"I hope he will be safe." She whispered.

"We will watch everything from here. If he needs our help, we will go to him." Rhamas promised.

The couple leaned into each other for a passionate kiss, then settled down where they thought they would have the best vantage point, and watched.

In less than thirty minutes, the squear could be seen leaving the cover of the forested hillside and stepping onto the grassy plain to begin his approach toward the city. Ahqui's motions were furtive – running for brief periods before flattening himself amid the vegetation to wait. There were times when even Alisha and Rhamas could not find him among the lush growths of grasses and weeds.

"There he is!" Alisha indicated a position no more than 100 feet from the first dome.

"Yes. I see him." Rhamas said. "There has been no magic trap?"

"I don't think so." Alisha answered. "But, sometimes, the alarms are silent. He is not out of danger until he is back in my arms."

"I can no longer see him." Rhamas announced. "We must pray that others will find him hard to spot as well." His arm draped across Alisha's shoulders and squeezed her to his side. It was at that moment that the city had come alive with flashing lights and sound.

"Ahqui!" Alisha got to her feet. "Has he been captured?"

"I cannot see!" Rhamas leaned forward to squint into the distance. "There are flying carts where he would have entered the city. There is some excitement happening – no doubt he has caused alarm."

"We must go now to help him!" Alisha pulled away from Rhamas and started to half-slide and half-run down the hillside, before she could be pulled up short by the strong grip of Rhamas's hand upon her garment.

"Stay with me, wife. We will watch. Ahqui is an animal – not a threat to them – even if they have managed to catch the creature – which I doubt Ahqui would allow – they will soon let him go."

Alisha must have seen the wisdom in his words, as she dropped to the ground again to watch the drama unfold in the distance. Her hands twisted the ends of her hair, and her teeth bit into her lower lip until a droplet of blood sat ruby-like against her skin.

"Look." Rhamas soothed her. "The flashing has

stopped, and the carts have flown away."

"I can still hear the..." Even as she started to say it, the blaring alarm cut off and left them with only the tiny night sounds of trees and insects. Coming, as it did, on the tail of such a frightening racket, the silence brought both relief and a sharp continuance of their suspense.

"Do you see him?" Alisha whispered, leaning to search the plain for Ahqui.

"Not yet." Rhamas said. "But, he will return. What reason could anyone have to detain him?"

His beautiful silver and white fur coat. Alisha thought. *His warm blood and sweet flesh.* She hugged herself, tightly.

The thoughts had occurred to both of them, simultaneously, but neither would give voice them.

From time to time there would be sightings – or so they hoped – but no true assurance that the squear was returning. Then, in a burst of unequaled joy, Ahqui could be seen leaving the grasses and diving back into the cover of the trees.

"There he is!" Rhamas cried.

"I see! I see!" Alisha wanted to scurry down the steep hillside to greet the squear, but soon saw the wisdom of staying put. "He's coming! He's safe. Oh, Rhamas."

Her face, in profile, was flushed and tearful, but it was clear to see that Alisha was overcome with relief at the safe return of her squear.

"It was good that we sent Ahqui. Do you see that, now? We would surely have been taken captive." Rhamas reminded her.

Alisha nodded, without taking her eyes from the approaching squear, but, even as she acknowledged the truth of his words, Alisha had given life to a vow that she would never endanger Ahqui in such a way again. Never.

Heavenly Bodies

In a reality far away, Skink floated lazily on a boogie board, watching the playful movements of sexy young women as they splashed in the waves or ran along the beach. His sunglasses were the reflective kind – not his favorite, but what had been the best fit at the swim shop. He hoped that his frank appraisals of the up-tilted breasts and flat, tanned tummies was being made less obvious behind the mirrored lenses.

They don't have girls like these where I come from. He thought, scanning the alluring gap between a pair of tanned thighs belonging to a fit blonde with a killer smile.

He allowed a series of waves to bring him closer to shore until he began to see the sand and shells through the clear-blue jewel of the sea. Skink put his feet down and walked the board out of the water and across the sand to the green and white beach umbrella that his parents were spread out under. He ran his hand through his hair like a comb and tried not to whip his head around in response to the vision of a curvy native girl who jogged by wearing an ankle bracelet of little golden shells and flowers.

"You done for the day?" His father asked, putting his book aside and picking up his beer.

"Me?" Skink laughed. "Done?"

Father and son exchanged a look that said everything. All of that half-naked female flesh had not gone unnoticed by his Dad, either.

Matthew (Skink) dropped his board and opened the cooler to get a Diet Coke. The pop-top fizz was one of his favorite sounds, and he had worked up a real thirst out there.

"She asleep?" Matthew asked.

Grant checked his wife and winced. "Uh-oh."

"Yep." Matthew shook his head. "She's a tad on the crispy side, wouldn't you say?"

"Honey? Honey? You need to wake up. You are going to get burnt." Grant liked to play things on the down-low side. No reason to alarm her, right?

Carolyn shifted slightly and raised her head. She shielded her eyes with her hand. "Should I flip over?" she asked.

Once again, the men exchanged looks. Matthew took

the lead.

"Gee, Mom." He said, picking up a towel and wrapping it around his shoulders. "I'm getting hungry. Think we could go back to the room for a while? Maybe shower and find some dinner somewhere?"

Carolyn sat up and dug her cell phone out of the beach bag. "What time is it?" She asked, trying to shade the screen enough to read it. "4:00? Really? Well, it's still early for dinner, but we can head back to the room, I guess." She looked at her tousled and gritty husband and smiled. He was starting to remind her of the man she had married. Sexy. "What do you think, handsome?" She winked at him provocatively – unaware of her lobster-like appearance and wild, untamed hair.

"I'm game. Maybe we can just hang out and watch a movie or something."

True to form, Matt's mother was consolidating their stuff before the verdict had even come in. Towels were shaken out and deposited in the bag she had brought for laundry. The cooler was latched and the trash was collected.

"You need to get that board back, right?" This to Matt, who was already stalking his way across the hot sand like a seven-foot flamingo. Then, Carolyn shouted after him, "Matt!

We'll meet you back at the room!"

Matthew didn't turn to acknowledge this last message, but flashed his Mom a backwards thumbs up, instead.

The hotel provided beach toys in exchange for room numbers, so all he had to do was drop the board off at the distribution cabana. On his way, he threaded through small groups of tantalizingly nubile women of all ages, and made up his mind to move to Hawaii at his first opportunity.

They had already been in Hawaii for over a week, but it hadn't seemed that way to Matthew. Back in Maryland, his buddies were attending trigonometry classes and hating life! He'd been purchasing and mailing postcards like mad – just to drive the fact home.

Wait until they see my candid shots! His grin widened, mischievously. Woo Hoo! *Life is good.*

That his Dad had been the one to come up with this idea was the oddest part of the trip. Already, he could see a miraculous transformation in his mother (not to mention her recent case of skin poisoning). He dropped off his board and looked back to watch his parents making their way across the sand. They were holding hands like lovers. Matthew followed that thought to its natural conclusion and grimaced.

Gross. He thought.

Matthew turned, ran his hand through his hair again, pinned it back by sliding his shades to the top of his head, and strode confidently to a row of open showers to rid himself of about a half-ton of white sand.

Not more than two feet in front of him, rinsing under the next shower head over, was another long-legged, model-type with one of those elegant braids running from the top of her head to the middle of her slightly arched back.

Mmm, mmm, mmmm. Life is good.

Return and Report

Ahqui was breathless and wide-eyed upon his return to the hilltop. Alisha had held out her arms to him, and he had made a bee-line for her lap where he trembled violently and whimpered for a time.

"Shh. Shh. Alisha is here. Ahqui is safe." She crooned.

Rhamas and Alisha exchanged worried glances. It was clear that whatever the little squear had observed in that city had frightened him half to death. Patting Ahqui gently while rocking him back and forth, Alisha's face was the very picture of guilt and remorse.

"We should never have sent him." She said. "The poor baby is terrified. It must have been awful for him."

"If we hadn't..." Rhamas began.

"I know. We might have been captured. We wouldn't have known about the alarm. I know it." She hugged Ahqui tightly to her chest. "Still, it wasn't fair to send him over there by himself. Anything could have happened."

"He is safe now." Rhamas assured her. "It might have

only been the loud sounds that frightened him; or the lights that were there and then not there so many times."

"Is there any water left?"

"A very little amount – I used everything in the stew."

"Can you get it for me? He is probably thirsty."

Rhamas rummaged through the packs and pulled out the flattened water skin. There wasn't enough left for more than a swallow, but he offered that to Ahqui who accepted it eagerly and whined for more.

The sun was on the horizon to herald a new day. As it rose, the lights of the city faded and died, leaving the vast arcs of glass open to the glaring reflections that threatened to stab Alisha's eyes and ricochet between the plates of her skull again. Alisha turned her back on the glare and put a hand over her eyes. Carefully, Alisha moved the slumbering Ahqui to a fur pallet and raised her arms over her head in a luxurious stretch.

"I can't feel my arms." She groaned.

Rhamas went behind Alisha to knead her back and shoulders with strong, callused hands.

"You need to rest. Please, lay down with him and sleep while I go to find water."

The eyes Alisha turned towards him were adamant. "Husband, we must stay together. I can bear no more worry."

Rhamas hesitated, but her expression and the anxiety in her movements caused him to relent. "Come then. Let us lay down together and rest. Perhaps Ahqui will feel well enough to search out water for us when he wakes."

Alisha smiled and sunk to the pallet with a sigh of exhaustion and relief. Rhamas curled his body against hers, and the three travelers slept while they could.

Ahqui was the first to wake a few hours later. He sought out Alisha's hands, grasped her fingers, and attempted to pull her upright.

"Errlisher! Errlisher!" He urged.

Alisha's eyes sprung open and she sat up. "Ahqui? Alisha was so worried about you. Come here to me." Ahqui entered the circle of her arms with a sigh before pointing urgently away from the city.

"You want us to run away? That place was very bad?" Alisha asked, gently.

The squear nodded vigorously and buried his face into her shoulder.

"Were they like Alisha? Were they human?"

A high whine escaped his throat and he shook his head.

"Did they touch you, Ahqui? Catch you?"

He shook his head again and began to tremble.

"We heard the loud noise and saw the lights. That was scary."

Ahqui leaned back a bit to meet her eyes. He made circles with his thumb and pointer finger and placed them over his eyes like a mask.

"Did they have big eyes?"

Again the nod and a quiver that shook him head to toe.

With a hand on her head, Alisha asked, "Were they big like Alisha, or little like Ahqui?"

Ahqui pointed to the sleeping Rhamas and held his hands far apart.

"Bigger than Rhamas?"

"Yes. Yes. Yes." The squear nodded. Then, Ahqui bent his arms and fingers into a claw-like stance, leaned forward, and began to come towards her with a pronounced lurching gait.

Alisha caught him and pressed Ahqui's body close to hers where she began to rock back and forth and croon softly to soothe his trembling.

"Rhamas? Rhamas?" She freed one of her hands to shake him. "Rhamas! We need to go from this place."

When his eyes came open, she could see that Rhamas also took a moment to realize where he was. His hair was tousled, and his chest was bare. Alisha felt the familiar flush of passion rising to her cheeks at the sight.

"What has happened?" He asked, pushing the blanket away as he sat up, and exposing more of his nakedness as he did so.

Alisha yanked her mind away from the awe of his nakedness, reluctantly, so that she could relay Ahqui's sense of urgency. "Ahqui is certain that we must move away from the city as soon as possible. He tells of bad, inhuman, creatures with huge eyes, that are much taller than even you, Rhamas."

"What makes them bad? Simply the fact that they are not human or Jurrah?" He asked.

"No." Alisha looked down at Ahqui. "I don't think that's it, anyway. Look at him, Rhamas, he is trembling with terror. He was sent there to tell us if it was a bad place, and we must weigh his impressions very heavily in our decision-making."

"Think what it would mean to have one of those magic

flying carts!" Rhamas urged. "We could move easily through this paclusin. Also, there is food in that city, and supplies that we will need."

And treasures. He thought to himself. *Magical treasures that can be found nowhere else."*

Alisha struggled to a standing position, and stood over him with the squear still clasped to her chest and its tail wrapped around her wrist. "I understand that you are curious, Rhamas." Ahqui whined and buried his face more deeply in Alisha's shoulder. "Perhaps the city is too dangerous for us at this time. Let us find water, and hunt for food as we leave this place. I promise to consider a search of one of the homesteads on our way. If, by some good fortune, we are able to befriend one of those creatures, then the city would become less of a threat."

Rhamas furrowed his brows and scratched his man parts. "Your plan sounds much like my own from the beginning of this place. Yes?"

Alisha rolled her eyes. "Yes. Yes, it does."

"But, now, my plan of watching the small houses is a good one?" His face lit up with a mischievous smile. "Is that what my wife says to me?"

"Yes, my husband. You are very wise. Can we please get ourselves away from this place, now? We have taken a great risk by coming so close."

Rhamas simply chuckled and nodded. He rose and went to slip his arms around Alisha's waist, but Ahqui wasn't having any of that, so Rhamas raised his hands up by way of surrender and went about finding his clothing and rolling up their packs.

Alisha bent to take up one of the bed rolls, but Ahqui would not allow himself to be put down, even for a minute, so Rhamas settled a pack over each shoulder, and the troupe began to pick their way down the wooded hillside.

Though it was not in his nature to show fear, it can be stated with surety that Rhamas did cast his eyes behind them at regular intervals. Whatever had frightened Ahqui had put the fear of God into him, and Rhamas wasn't anxious to share in that experience.

The travelers kept away from the road upon their return – prepared to duck behind trees or outcroppings of rock should a car go whizzing by. While four of these did pass – (two red, one green, and one black) – Rhamas and Alisha felt certain that they had not been seen.

Ahqui sniffed out another water station a few hours into their journey and they drank as much of the fresh water as they could hold – pouring bowls full of it over their heads to cool off once their thirsts had been quenched. The weather had been very warm, and their leather tunics and pants had been unsuitable. Once every water skin had been filled, the party walked onward throughout the afternoon and well into the evening.

Rhamas found a shallow cave in which they could shelter for the night, and set a pot of soup over a fire. This was to be a pale comparison to the feast of the night before, however, as it was made with vegetables only, and such seasonings as Rhamas had been able to gather. Still, it filled their bellies and allayed their fears enough to allow the exhausted trio a restful night's sleep.

Within the shelter of the dank-smelling cave, Alisha began to dream. She found herself trying to escape from the dark interior of the house of the Agrigar Wise Man. Her fingers struggled with the dozens of latches and chains that held the door fast, but – for every lock she managed to open – another would appear in its place!

The smell of a grave filled Alisha's nose and mouth so thickly that it was difficult to catch her breath, and then, from deep inside the house there were footsteps coming towards her. Strong, confident strides. The Wise Man with his horrible, staring eyes! He would catch her! With this terrifying realization, Alisha had redoubled her efforts to break free. She worked her fingers to bloody stubs sliding, turning, unlatching and lifting any locks that appeared.

Then, with a mighty shudder, the door swung wide and Alisha escaped! The sky outside was bright and blue, and Alisha ran! The air that filled her lungs was sweet with the fragrance of freshly-mown grass, and she could feel the lawn under her feet! Cool, spongy and green – just like it had been at home.

Home. I'm home!

Everything swirled and twisted within her vision, and, when the scene had finally cleared, Alisha found herself in Maryland. The house was white with hunter green shutters and a matching door. In every aspect, the house was as she remembered it. Her home!

The door loomed up in front of her and Alisha gripped the doorknob and attempted to enter, but the knob refused to turn. The door was locked up tight.

Alisha banged against it with both fists, hollering ...

"Skink! Mom! Dad! It's me! I'm back! I'm home! Open the door! Mom? LET ME IN!"

Sitting straight up, Alisha crowned her head on the ceiling of the cave and cried out in pain.

"My wife!" Rhamas called out in alarm. "What has happened? Are you hurt?"

Alisha did not answer, but mashed her hands down on the newly-forming lump to quiet the pain while tears of frustration ran down her cheeks.

"My love?" Rhamas was at her side, then – peeling aside her hands to examine the injury to her head. "Isssch!" He said. "You have made a bump. I think you bleed, but it is too dark to see well."

Alisha let the edges of her dream become tattered and fly away in brightly-colored strips. She accepted a moistened cloth from Rhamas and pressed it to the lump with a wince.

"Is that better?"

"I guess so. It hurts."

"Please, come and lay down with me." Rhamas urged. "Morning is yet a long way off."

Slowly, and with great care, Alisha did lie down again at

her husband's side. And, though she did eventually fall back to sleep, she did not dream.

Memories of Love

Carolyn sat on the balcony of their suite watching the sun come up over a jewel-blue sea. A cool breeze caused her to pull her satin robe close around her shoulders. Some surfers were already at it, though Grant and Matthew were still sound asleep.

It is so beautiful here. She thought. *So quiet and...*

"Peaceful, isn't it?" Grant joined her, closing the French doors quietly behind himself.

"Yes." She gave him her hand as he came to sit beside her. "I was just thinking that very thing."

"We needed this." He said.

"I haven't thanked you, yet, have I?" Carolyn smiled. "For bringing us here, I mean. For canceling all of your appointments and..."

"Like I said, we *needed* this!" He interrupted. "I was no good for anything at the office, feeling the way I did, and worrying about you."

"Well, thank you. It has been a wonderful help to my spirits – and, I could be wrong, but I think our son is making the most of things, as well." She winked.

"Like father, like son. Isn't that the way it goes?"

"I am happy to see him show an interest in girls." Carolyn added. "Do you think he'll start dating someday soon?"

"All things happen in their time. He has never been quick to start up a conversation, you know."

"Very true."

"Unlike Alisha, who could strike up a debate with a fence post." Grant laughed, remembering how Alisha had learned to talk and never stopped, since.

Carolyn looked away and blinked back some quiet tears, which began a period of comfortable silence between them, filled with memories of all that they had been to each other – all of the joys and all of the suffering – the loss…

"She would have loved this so much." Carolyn allowed herself to smile. "Especially, if we had been able to wrest the book from her hands and force her out of the suite!"

Grant chuckled. "She wasn't much of an adventurer, our girl."

"She was nervous about going away to college, you know."

"Yes."

"She didn't have any idea what she wanted to do with her life. She could have done so many things."

Grant squeezed his wife's hand and met her eyes. "She could have done anything and made a complete success of it."

"I want to believe she is still alive, Grant." Carolyn sighed.

"We need to believe that she is okay." He agreed. "Either here, or in heaven."

Silence descended again. Their hands formed a bridge for shared memories of their enigmatic, opinionated, and strong-willed daughter. The first to appear at mealtimes, and the last to turn out her lamp at night, Alisha's serious, rosy-cheeked face asking wild questions about Unicorns and Faeries, her eyes gone wide as she listened to their answers.

"Remember when she cornered us about that car?" They both laughed out loud.

"Oh, yes."

'It is only like $400, and Skink said he'd fix it like new for

a couple hundred more, and…'

Grant continued in his deeper imitation of Alisha's impassioned plea. *'If you loan me the money now, I'll have it all paid back by the time school starts. No joke, Dad. Every single penny!'*

"I can't believe I let her buy that piece of junk." Grant looked down, and wiped a tear from his eye. "But, darn it, if she wasn't cute standing there with that determined look on her face."

"She paid you back, didn't she?"

"That, she did." He said. "That, she did."

"Well, if we ever see her again on this earth, let's lock her bedroom door and throw away the key!" Carolyn laughed a bit tearfully.

"It's a deal!" Grant said, pounding his fist on the other arm of his chair. "Better than that! I'll build a tower to the clouds with only one window, and tell her to start growing out her hair."

"I miss her so much." She cried. "I just need to see her one more time before I die."

"No problem praying for that. We will just have to keep her in our hearts until then." Grant said.

Matthew rested his hand on the door to the balcony, but didn't open it. His parents' voices had come to him easily enough, and he hadn't wanted to interfere. Yet, through the glass panes, he sent his memories and his feelings of loss to mingle with those of his parents, and for the first time since Alisha disappeared, Matthew cried.

Clearing the Air

When the first homestead appeared against the tree-line, Rhamas brought the group to a stop. "There. Are we to approach it by day, or by night?"

Ahqui registered his disapproval by pedaling his feet in mid-air and trying to claw his way to the ground, and Alisha was forced to allow him. As soon as the squear's hind feet hit the dirt, Ahqui crossed his arms and fixed them both with a determined set to his face that was almost humorous before shaking his head in an emphatic "No!" and staring them down.

Rhamas looked at Alisha.

"I can tell you that we won't be sending Ahqui over there by himself." She said, too loudly.

"And, I agree with you." Rhamas gave a nod to the squear, who answered it with a convincing attempt at a "harrumph!"

"How far away is the Ghama Traya?" She asked. "A two-hour sprint? A one-hour gallop?"

"Much farther than that." Rhamas answered, crossing his arms, as well. "What difference does it make? Those things have cars. We couldn't hope to outrun them."

"We need a plan for escape before I'll agree to try anything."

Rhamas seemed to take Alisha's statement to heart. His head was bent and he turned to scan the surroundings for any possible hiding spots.

"Do you see anywhere to hide?" He asked, impatiently. Once we cross the road, we will be in plain sight."

"You really want to see what's in there, don't you?" She quipped. "Is this to be another campfire tale for your Jurrah brethren?"

At Rhamas's unexpected silence, she continued. "Aha! Rhamas the Explorer must not be seen to run from the city in fear! Is that it?"

The face that Rhamas turned upon her was filled with shame and anger. Alisha was moved backward by the unexpected force of his emotion. "Rhamas?" He turned his back to her and stomped away. "My love?"

Alisha caught up to Rhamas and let her hands rest gently on his shoulders. "My husband, Rhamas? Please do not feel anger towards me. I was only playing with words. I had no thought of hurting you."

"You play with words too much, my wife." Rhamas grumbled, still refusing to face her. "You say, 'bullshit' to me, and you talk much of things I have not seen and have no knowledge of. Never did you talk of these things in the village. You were all innocent fawn, lost and afraid and in need of husband and protector. I think now that you played many word games with me and my people."

She was taken aback by his accusation. Alisha, for once, was unable to speak.

Rhamas turned to face her and, in doing so, dislodged her hands from his shoulders. "Do you see me as weak and slow, now? Do you think me a joke to laugh in front of?"

"Rhamas. I..." Alisha gulped.

"Do you not trust me to protect you from what lives in that glass house, there?" He pointed at the dome. "Am I not strong? Can I not lead you in safety? Please tell me these things, Alisha. Many nights I lay awake wondering these things. I am tired now of wondering. Will I be your protector, or will you be mine?"

Alisha was stunned. She felt like crying, but no tears

would come. Rhamas stood waiting for a reply, and she was not even able meet his eyes.

How could I not have seen this happening? Alisha's mind raced. *Of course, he's never seen lights or cars or glass... Have I made him feel stupid? Have I failed to trust in his judgment? Clearly, I have. He is telling me how I have made him feel.* She felt her cheeks flush with shame.

Alisha's mind explored the actions and words that had made up their time together, and, like a tongue refusing to leave the sharp edge of a broken tooth, Alisha was forced to agree that she had treated her husband with a lack of respect on many occasions. She had dismissed his wonder over the beautiful roadways as childish ignorance, she had accused him of killing the baby rabbits out of cruelty, and she had rebuked him for allowing Ahqui to check out the city first – even though his suggestion might actually have saved their lives.

"Husband." The barely-audible whisper escaped her lips. "I have behaved badly. I did not think it, but, now..."

Rhamas could plainly see that his new wife was struggling to grasp the impact of her poorly-chosen statements. He went to her, and lifted her chin until their eyes met. "Wife. I have accused you, wrongly. I see that your heart has honor towards me."

Alisha nodded and slipped, willingly, into his arms. "Rhamas. I..."

"There is no need to talk further, my wife. I was cross with you, but that has passed."

As they walked, hand-in-hand, Alisha took the opportunity to explain herself.

"Rhamas, when I followed the Agrigars into their village, I was freezing and hungry and hadn't seen any living creature other than Ahqui in many weeks. The Agrigars frightened me, but I knew I would surely die if I was forced to spend the winter on my own."

"Tell me you were never afraid of the root people!" He teased.

"But, I was! They were like nothing I had ever seen before -- and those horrible eyes..."

"That they are open always?"

Alisha nodded. "Then, I met the Jurrah. They were so much like me, that I was no longer frightened. They took me in, bathed me, clothed and fed me."

"It is the way of my people to give shelter to any in need

of it." Rhamas's voice conveyed a quiet pride.

"Maryland has many wondrous things of which you are ignorant – that is true. But, I was as a baby in your world, and you taught me all that was needed. I came to love the Jurrah way of life, and also to love you. I could have lived there – beside you – for all of the days left to me."

"Shh. Let us talk of this no more." He led her back into the shadows of the forest and beckoned for Ahqui to follow, which he did, although with a certain degree of indignation.

Once they had found a place of shelter that was a safe distance from the road, the water was brought out and the party refreshed themselves. Alisha unfolded a piece of white leather and began to draw upon it with burning embers.

Rhamas looked at the image that was taking shape under the embers. "This is the Ghama Traya?"

Alisha smiled. "Yes. I am marking the places we have touched, and joining them to pictures of the worlds they have taken us to."

He leaned closer to look. "I see this. It is good to have a way to remember." Rhamas paused. "Which place do I touch to go home again?"

Alisha pointed at a place on the drawing. "This one

brought us from Natalo I to where we are now." She explained. "I believe that touching it again will take us back, but I can't be certain. That is the way it worked between Natalo I and Natalo II."

He sat beside her and looked puzzled. "Do you believe that touching there will take me home from any world, or just from this one?"

Alisha's head was spinning. "I don't know. This is very confusing. It may take us a lifetime to figure it out."

"That is fine." He said. "We have a lifetime to figure it out together."

He leaned in and kissed her on the cheek, then on the mouth. "Why are all of these paclusins on the same land? The same trees and plains and valleys?"

Alisha thought about the question and – only then – did she realize the truth of his observation. Though each reality had evolved in a different direction, the landscapes surrounding the Ghama Traya had been similar.

"You are wise to have seen such, as that knowledge never came to me." She admitted. "I am not sure why these realities exist, Rhamas. It has been explained to me that they are side-by-side, like the layers of an onion. Most beings are never aware of any reality but the one in which they were born."

"If they are next to each other, but in the same place," he paused, scratching his head. "Then, how does this world have four moons, and my world only one?"

Silence stretched between them as the questions seemed endless and the answers so out of reach.

Alisha sighed. "Different things happened in each reality to make them the way they are. There is much in every existence that we will not understand. I think we will always long for our homes, and the surroundings that feel most natural to us."

"I am longing for my home over the mountains." Rhamas admitted, in a near whisper. "I wish to begin our life together there. We have seen many great things, wife, but it tires me to walk and walk, but never arrive home."

As the sun went down, there were deep kisses and passionate lovemaking while Ahqui pretended to nap in the lower branches of an evergreen tree. The crackling of dying embers was the only sound.

Meeting Xiri

Ahqui opened one eye and scanned the campsite. He had heard footsteps, hadn't he? Smelled something strange, yet oddly familiar? From his position, half-way up an evergreen tree, he could just make out something tall, impossibly thin and transparent.

Ahqui's ruff stood out from his neck and his bowels emptied as he leapt bravely from his hiding place to land, squarely, on the invader's stooped shoulders and upper back.

"Errlisherrr!!" Ahqui growled and spat. "Errlisherr!!"

The trespasser sang out in fear and pain as the squear ripped and tore at its back and limbs. It was a resonant, vibrating tone that continued to jump octaves until the sound had become unbearably shrill.

Rhamas and Alisha jumped to their feet and tried to make sense of what they were seeing.

"What is that, thing?" Alisha had to yell to be heard above the fight.

"It must be one of them." Rhamas answered. "It is made

of glass, yes?"

"Or, something very much like it." Alisha admitted, crouched to fight.

Something about the creature's cries caused Rhamas to lunge forward and sweep Ahqui from its back with one movement of his muscled arm. The squear flew several feet to land with a "thud" on the forest floor.

Alisha, following her husband's lead, caught the militant squear up in her arms and held him back – a decision which left her covered with bites and scratches, as Ahqui was bound to save them – whether they wanted it or not.

"Shh. Ahqui! Shh. You have done well to warn us, Ahqui. You must stop now." Alisha turned her back on the creature and carried the squear out of the trees and into the clearing in an effort to calm him.

Once Rhamas had successfully removed its assailant, he tried to offer the being assistance by sharing his water flask and speaking calmly and slowly. The Alien's screeching tones lowered by octaves before stopping altogether, though it did not accept the flask.

"Are you hurt?" Alisha asked, finally. "We are very sorry. Ahqui is trained to protect us while we sleep. As you can see, he is very well-trained."

The interloper's eyes were huge and very black. When they moved within their orbits, a small white pupil could be seen to track with them. Their black surfaces glittered with moisture. It looked at them, now, but made no sound. Its fingers were long and insect-like, as were its very long legs, and all of them as clear as icicles.

Alisha thought it resembled a praying mantis from her reality, except that it had two back legs, instead of four, and no wings. She tried to discern whether this was a male or a female, but soon gave up – feeling it rude to stare very long.

Rhamas sat down, and indicated for Alisha to do the same. As hoped, the alien being folded up its legs to sit also. Its impossibly long arms folded in front of its body as if in prayer. Ahqui started to whine, but Alisha did her best to quiet him.

"Eeee wupwup - Eeee Wupup." The alien replied.

"We are travelers from another place," said Alisha with a soothing voice. "We want to be friends with your people."

Silence. The triangular head bent sideways and the pupils rolled oddly from one of them to the next in consideration.

As soon as it was certain that it was no longer under attack, it lowered one shoulder and tried to peer at its injuries while the other arm prodded at rents and scratches in its flesh.

"Oooo ett ett - Oooo ett ett." The creature cried, plaintively.

"Rhamas? Can you help it? Make some pain goo, or something?" Alisha whispered.

"I can try." He agreed, doubtfully. "But, who knows whether it will help or do harm to such a one as this?"

"We have to try." Alisha urged. Then, to the mantis, she said. "Awww ooo ett ett."

The very large eyes rolled back to look at her, while the head and shoulder squared to attention. To Alisha, this meant that her attempt at communication had gained the creature's interest, if not its understanding.

Rhamas pulled a crooked brown tuber from his bag of herbs and began to mash it between two rocks.

"Hurry!" Urged Alisha.

Rhamas shot her a warning glance and continued to work. He scraped the white substance that had oozed from the tuber onto his knife, and then transferred it to his hands.

"Aww ett ett - Aww ett ett - Aww ett ett"

Alisha and Rhamas looked at the alien with

astonishment to hear the phrase repeated so perfectly.

"I heard it, but I don't believe it," murmured Rhamas.

The alien worked its insect-like mouth and said it again – this time much louder and up a full octave. "Aww ett ett - Aww ett ett - Aww ett ett."

"Do you have some of that ready, yet?" Alisha whispered.

"Yes." He said. "Who is going to . . ?"

"I'll try. What do I have to do?"

"Smooth this over the injuries to help the pain." He said, adding, "Carefully!"

"Aww help help?" Alisha repeated as she made a very slow approach.

The creature flinched away from Alisha – just a bit – before settling down and allowing her to walk behind it and gently apply the salve.

"Aww help help - Aww help help - Aww help help" the alien intoned, gratefully.

Rhamas and Alisha exchanged relieved glances and took their first full breaths since having been awakened by the altercation.

Ahqui had climbed to the top of a tree, but wasn't missing a thing.

Alisha finished applying the salve and reached down to touch the creature's hand. The glistening eyes followed Alisha's motions with extreme caution, but did nothing to intercept her touch.

"Alisha Alisha Alisha." She said, pointing to herself

"Alisha Alisha Alisha." The thing repeated.

At her nod, Rhamas followed suit. "Rhamas Rhamas Rhamas" He said, also pointing at himself.

"Rhamas Rhamas Rhamas." Again, the creature seemed to understand.

Then, it stretched one of its long arms almost to the point of touching the tree that Ahqui was hiding in and cried: "Oooo ett ett - Oooo ett ett - Ooo ett ett!"

A fierce growl could be heard from within the branches, but not a single molecule of actual squear was available for introduction.

The clear appendage reached that much further and tapped the tree only slightly, causing it to topple to the ground with an enormous 'WHUMPH!' and exposing a huddled and wide-eyed squear where once the tree had been.

"That is Ahqui." Laughed Alisha.

"Ahqui Ahqui Ahqui." It announced, proudly. "Ahqui."

Then, the squear fainted.

Xiri of Montaroon

Though their relationship hadn't gotten off to the best start, Xiri seemed quick to forgive the travelers and to exhibit an almost exhaustive curiosity about Ahqui. She wanted to carry him, (very much, apparently, as she kept reaching out towards the squear and repeating his name in sets of three). Ahqui had taken to riding on Rhamas's shoulders for the time being, however, and wasn't having any of that.

Xiri was a female, and – after much pointing and repetition – found to be a member of the Minnach people. Her mate, Xartu, and her daughter, Xanxi lived in the first red-domed homestead south of the City of Piscine.

Xartu was taller than Xiri and broader across the shoulders by a good deal. Xanxi on the other hand, was small and opaque (The clarity – as with human children – did not manifest until well after puberty). None of the Minnach possessed so much as a single hair, or were bothered at all by nudity. If they had sexual parts, they were not immediately evident, and Alisha didn't ask.

The hardest part of hanging with the Minnach was the fact that their transparent exoskeleton left their internal organs constantly on display. Alisha found this almost hypnotically fascinating.

Minnach viscera came in a vivid array of colors and were connected by endless loops and swirls of green and yellow tubing that ushered bits of this and that from one unidentifiable organ to another with a swoosh of bubbling fluid -- much reminiscent of the funky lava and bubble lamps of the Earth 70's. (This, as you can imagine, made it impossible to have any kind of an intelligent conversation after lunch).

The dome itself was gorgeous beyond understanding. It was of a deepest ruby red that swathed everything inside with a warm and rosy glow. There was a vaulted ceiling, (high enough to give five Rhamas's standing on each other's shoulders to engage in spirited calisthenics without danger of splitting his skull), and simple, cubistic furnishings and appliances that were carved out in spots to accommodate their impossibly scrawny behinds.

Minnach lived off of birds and fish for the most part, explaining the interesting way in which all of the waterways had been capped off by watering stations and allowed to flow underground into dozens of fisheries (blue domes) that could be seen dotting the countryside. Birds were raised within yellow domes, exclusively – thus, the dearth of fine-feathered-friends in the trees, meadows and hillsides of Montaroon.

Rhamas, Alisha and Ahqui were served huge portions of delicious fishes and fowl, which their starved bodies appreciated, enormously. The sauces and gravies were delightful in their piquancy, and spices rare, and unusual, had been sprinkled throughout.

This home provided the first opportunity for Rhamas to witness the wonder of indoor plumbing. He had scratched his head at the genius of it, and couldn't wait to return home someday to introduce the technology to his people.

"This is so simple for small children!" He had exclaimed. "Why has this not been done by the Jurrah?"

"The Jurrah have a lapa for washing." Alisha noted.

"Yes." Rhamas nodded, still deep in thought. "When we return to my people, I will do this thing and they will be held wisest among tribes."

Alisha wondered if there would ever come a time when they would be welcome to rejoin the Jurrah, but didn't share her thoughts. After all, even the Agrigar had marked them as criminals and fugitives... She changed the subject.

"Do you still want to see the domed city, Rhamas?"

He shifted his weight and looked away. "There is time for that, my wife. We can visit this paclusin with one touch of a red rock. If you wish it, we can try again to reach your home of Maryland."

Alisha reached out to sweep the hair out of his eyes. "I love you, husband. You honor me with these words. I would very much like to go home again."

He swept her up in his arms and swung her full circle, causing her to squeal with surprise and alarming Ahqui and their insectile-ish hosts.

"Whee!" He said, by way of explanation. Little Anxi caught his meaning quickly – despite her childish opacity – and translated it into Minnach.

"Aish! Aish! Aish!" She said, and everybody smiled.

The Cart with no Oxen

After a generous breakfast of fried fish and eggs, Rhamas asked Xartu about the city, and how they – as strangers from another place – might be received there. Xartu pushed his plate to one side and seemed to think deeply before making a reply.

"Octoo Buron Octoo." He had both hands raised with palms facing Rhamas as he said this. "Octoo Buron Octoo."

"What do you think he is saying?" Rhamas murmured to Alisha, who was sitting on his left. "Was that a 'yes' or a 'definitely not?'"

"It looks like 'stop' to me." Alisha replied. "I guess that would be a 'no'."

Xiri cleared the table with a worried demeanor. Xanxi nervously groomed her head, eyes and mouth (much the way a housefly would).

"Buron?" Alisha tried.

Little Xanxi stood to her full height, picked up something

that resembled a broom, and rested it on her shoulder before beginning to march around the table with a menacing look on her face.

"She is saying that the city is occupied by soldiers." Alisha guessed.

"Soldiers with weapons and no happy faces, eh?" Rhamas raised one eyebrow.

Alisha patted little Xanxi and nodded her head. The pantomimed message had come through loud and clear.

"That explains Ahqui's warnings." This from Alisha, who had picked up some of the dirty dishes and taken them to Xiri. "So, the city will have to wait for another time. Perhaps we can convince them to give us a ride to the next watering station, though. Do you want to give it a try?"

"This is not a gift I have." He said. "Their language is not in my mouth."

"I think I can make Xiri understand, but, now that I have seen how tall they are, I wonder if there will be enough room in that thing for all of us."

Ahqui was still chomping handfuls of breakfast when Alisha motioned for Xiri to walk outside. Rhamas, curious, followed the two women out into the morning sun – he was instantly hit with a wall of scorching heat and the smell of toasting dirt.

How does the dome stay so cool under such a sun? He wondered.

He found Alisha and Xiri standing next to the flying cart and waving their arms around in an attempt to communicate more effectively. Alisha pointed at herself, and the flying cart. Xiri was holding up her palms and looking distressed.

"Octoo Buron Octoo." Xiri repeated again.

Alisha shook her head and pointed away from the city and back in the direction in which they had come. "Water?" She tried without much hope, and even less success.

Rhamas ducked back inside the dome and pulled his water flask out of his pack. When he approached the women again, he poured some over Alisha's hands.

"Water?" Alisha said again.

"Rauntu Rauntu!" Xiri's face lit with understanding and she pointed behind her to the place Alisha had indicated.

Alisha nodded and smiled. "Rauntu."

It was now Xiri's turn to return to the dome. Once inside, she beckoned her mate with words that were strange to them and were surprised when Xartu placed his hand upon the flying cart and climbed into the resulting opening with an expectant look upon his face.

Alisha walked forward, placed her hand on the cool surface of the car, and climbed in beside him.

"He will take us, Rhamas!" She said. "Gather up our things and call Ahqui? It is time to go."

Rhamas slung the two packs over his shoulders and held his arms out for Ahqui. The squear eyed him, suspiciously, but did eventually drop from his chair and waddle over to be lifted.

Rhamas was both excited and afraid. To ride in the flying cart without oxen through heaven was a story beyond any Jurrah's wildest imaginings. He had seen them moving swiftly along the glass roads, and had wished to be inside – flying like a without wings or feathers. He thought of his home now, and not for the first time. He wanted to teach his people about inside water coming from outside, and tell them of his journey inside the Paclusin of Montaroon.

He imagined his mother's face when he had failed to return with the others to their village and her shame when stories of his thieving and running away had come to her ears.

She would learn of his wedding to a human girl, and grieve the fact that she had not been there to witness the marriage of her only son.

It is less difficult to know Alisha's need, as my heart begins to long for home, as well.

Xiri came to the car with a bundle of food and supplies. One of her impossibly long – praying-mantis-type arms passed this gift to where Alisha sat inside the vehicle.

"Quinxa Alisha Quinxa." Xiri said.

"Quinxa Xiri Quinxa." Alisha replied with warmth and gratitude for Xiri's friendship.

Rhamas had to grasp the struggling Ahqui firmly to get him into the car. The squear was not too keen on new experiences – this was a knowledge hard-won from many thrashings, scratchings and undesirable defecations, so Rhamas held the beast at arm's length and passed him off to Alisha at his first opportunity.

Seated within the black egg, Alisha felt quite at home. Though small inside, it wasn't unlike her mother's Subaru. The two-day walk to the Ghama Traya had been looming over her like a black spider on a fine silk thread. It seemed to Alisha as though they had been hiking for months, and her body had been pushed to its breaking point. She took in a deep breath and relaxed in her seat. She had missed the luxury of a car more than she had realized.

Rhamas and Ahqui were less at ease. Though, Alisha did her best to comfort the 'boys,' the whirring sound, the lurching into full speed, and the landscape racing past their windows soon had the car filled with the smell of Ahqui's offal and Rhamas's whispered prayers.

Xartu turned his head, twice, to look for the source of the stench, and his shoulders stiffened visibly with irritation.

My squear just shit in his new car. Alisha thought, ruefully. *I will have to clean it up when we get to the watering station. I wish I knew how to say 'I'm sorry my squear shit in your new car, and I will clean it up at the watering station.'* But, she didn't, and it made for an unbearably quiet ride.

The countryside swept past them through heavily-tinted windows, and Rhamas was soon able to open his eyes to the moving vista with wonder. The car moved over the road so smoothly that – had they closed their eyes – the travelers would have sworn they had not been moving at all.

For Alisha, the novelty of this new mode of transportation was short-lived, and her anticipation was built around the possibility of reaching Maryland and reuniting with her family. What would they do when they saw her walking up to the house? She smiled.

They are going to tackle me and squish me with hugs and kisses and declarations of love... She let the images fill her mind and a smile came to her lips. "*Mom will make meatloaf and mashed potatoes – my favorite – and Skink will reveal my perfectly renovated Pontiac...*

Alisha was so deep within her reveries, that she hadn't noticed when the car had come to a stop.

"My wife." Rhamas put his hand on her knee. "We have arrived."

The group piled out of the glass egg and stretched their arms and legs. The quarters had been tight, but nobody dared complain as the car had saved them miles of hiking under the hot sun.

Alisha made a face and pointed to the mess that her squear had made in the car.

Xartu bowed his head and shrugged, as if to say the mess was 'no big deal.'

"Rhamas, can you get my old shirt out of the pack, please?"

Alisha took the rag to the watering station and lifted the dome. She wet the rag and squeezed out the excess water before climbing into the car and starting to wipe away the sludge.

Xartu made polite noises that were easily understood to mean "Please, don't bother with the mess. I will clean it up later." But, Alisha took note of the fact that he made no move stop her as she made repeated trips to the basin to rinse out the yellow-green feces.

Alisha worked at the sludgy stains until there was no trace of squear poo to be found, and offered her thanks and apologies to Xartu with hand motions and smiles.

The large-eyed alien nodded, bowed slightly, and climbed back into his car with a sigh of relief. In less than a moment, the car was gone from their view and the small troupe was left alone to ponder their next move.

The Ghama Traya was only a short walk up the rise from the little clearing where they now settled in for the night. And, just as she had done before, Alisha plopped Ahqui into the basin of clear water and scrubbed him until he squealed (which wasn't very long at all).

Their dreams that night were vivid and as different as

snowflakes. Rhamas dreamed of flying cars, Jurrah children gathered at his feet to hear of his adventures, and a long-overdue reunion with his mother.

Alisha drove her '64 Pontiac Catalina through wispy purple clouds to the set of Oprah where she displayed Rhamas and Ahqui in matching tuxes to the free world. Ahqui was very dashing in a tux – her sleeping mind surmised.

Ahqui, for his part, dreamed of breakfast, lunch and dinner as he lay on his back like a beached whale with his arms and legs akimbo. His fur had dried into an embarrassing state of fluffiness that had given him an adorable squishy teddy bear appearance. Thankfully, he had fallen to sleep before taking notice of it. Fluffiness made Ahqui very cross.

Developer's Nightmare

Oliver Wyndham was a well-dressed man of medium height with a full head of wavy hair and a bulbous, red-veined nose.

There was something off about his hair.

It had been dyed such a severe shade of black that he more closely resembled a middle-aged man in a plastic helmet than a much younger version of himself (as he had hoped).

Mr. Wyndham now stood planted in a large field of decapitated corn stalks, looking irritated.

Smack dab in the center of the property was an ugly, red rock. Oliver had purchased the land cheaply, as it had been part of a divorce settlement, and both parties had been anxious to walk away with equal shares of cash and have done with it.

He reached for his cell phone and kicked at a clod of dried dirt.

The fields had once grown corn and pumpkins and been the site of a popular local attraction every autumn. A corn maze.

Hay ride. Pumpkins for kiddies. Stuff like that. Oliver had his general contractor's number on speed dial, and pressed the "3."

Nice family they had been, by all accounts.   Divorce was such a shame. Still, their misfortune was his windfall, right?

"Pete?" Oliver covered his mouth to cough. "Yah. Listen, that Maryland property off Webber Junction that I've been talking about?" He coughed again and wondered if he ought to consider kicking his 4-pack-a-day habit. "Yah. There's a great sodding rock in the middle of it, and it's gotta' go."

A cold wind came up on an otherwise warm and windless day, and Oliver considered leaning against the boulder for shelter, but stepped away from it and pulled his jacket tighter around him, instead. It was just an obstacle and an eyesore – a bulky mass of compressed sediment – but it gave Oliver a creepy feeling. He chuckled at himself for being such an ass and tried to concentrate instead on his associate's scheduling restrictions.

"Look, Pete." He said, making confident strides towards his silver BMW. "These houses have got to go up lickety-f-ing-split, got that? Tomorrow. Yah. I need you and a bull dozer out here by 8:00 a.m., or I'll find somebody else to do it. Lots of guys out there with bull dozers. You'd be surprised."

Oliver thrust his hand into a pants pocket and retrieved his remote.

"Yah. Damn thing is probably 5' tall, and just about as big around!" Mr. Wyndham listened for a moment, and then burst in. "I don't know how far down it goes, how much it weighs, or how you're going to get it out. Just bring everything you've got and clear it away. Turn it into gravel for all I care."

The voice emanating from his cell took on a more conciliatory tone, and Oliver's face shone victorious.

Well, I'll see you there, or know the reason why." He ended the call abruptly, returned the phone to his jacket and coughed again,

An elegant tone unlocked the BMW and he climbed into the buttery-leather seat and drove off thinking about cigarettes and money, divorce and lung disease in equal measures. He was a busy guy. Busy guys were always thinking.

Going Home, at Last

Breakfast was made up of the provisions given to them as a farewell gift from Xiri – some small roasted birds and dried fish. Alisha and Rhamas ate quietly as they faced the endless possibilities facing them at the Ghama Traya. Each hoped that "home" would be their next destination, but both knew, by now, that anything expected was unlikely.

Ahqui rubbed his eyes as he pushed a handful of dried fish into his mouth. He had been accustomed to travel with his other human companion, but hadn't been required to jump realities with such alarming frequency and forced to befriend such terrifying beings into the bargain. The journey was making him fat – not lean and muscular as one would imagine. He often traveled via Alisha or Rhamas, and was rarely given the freedom to wander about on his own.

Alisha lifted a pack to her shoulder before bending down to gather up the squear. Rhamas washed his face and hands in the clear basin before filling up all of the water skins.

"Are you ready to tour the next paclusin?" Alisha asked, wryly.

Rhamas smiled. "Ah, yes. How much more wondrous will the next one be? Will we eat or be eaten? I dare not wait another moment to find out."

"We agree that we will try many places until we reach Maryland today?"

"This Maryland, I must see to believe." He answered. "Will there be many lovely women there in silly shoes?"

"There will be women, yes, but, none for your eyes to follow, my husband."

Rhamas slid his arms around her waist and kissed her forehead and cheek before finding her lips with his. Ahqui – who sat between them in Alisha's arms – made his feelings known and they separated with laughter.

"Perhaps, we should have given this beast to little Xanxi as a gift? Surely, he becomes tired of our inappropriate behavior."

Ahqui took no notice of his comment – if, indeed, he had been able to grasp its meaning. Instead, he turned his head to bury it in Alisha's shoulder and grasped hold of her garment with both hands as was his custom.

The three of them walked silently through the quiet morning to the Ghama Traya. It was a small distance, yet they found themselves unwilling to hurry. Though they were becoming accustomed to portal travel, it was still a very humbling thing to contemplate.

"If we find ourselves somehow back in Natalo I?" Rhamas asked, in a whisper.

"Would you wish to stay?" Alisha stopped and turned to face him.

Rhamas nodded. "We could cross the mountains to my people, and I believe we would find acceptance there."

"So soon? I do not agree. How would we pass unseen by the Agrigars?"

He looked at his feet before meeting her eyes. "I have been a long time from my home. Winter among the Agrigars was uncomfortable, but necessary. I now understand how you miss the things you know – the people you know..."

"Yes." She agreed, turning once again towards the Ghama Traya. "There is no place like home."

Rhamas missed the smile that warmed her face as she gave life to those words from "The Wizard of Oz."

Dorothy had ruby slippers and a hot-air balloon, and I have a pair of flip-flops and honking great rock. She mused. *How fair is that?*

Alisha thought about arriving home and hitting the mall for some new clothes and shoes. The weather had been growing increasingly warmer, and the leather tunics, pants and boots were no longer cutting it. She couldn't help wondering what Rhamas would think of the mall. She would have to stop at Cinnabon®, Orange Julius®, and Auntie Anne's Pretzels☺, too, of course.

Her thoughts left her standing at the base of the Ghama Traya. Rhamas stood behind her with his hands on her hips, and his chin resting on one shoulder.

"Where will you take us this time, lovely one?" He planted kisses on her neck that gave her goosebumps up both arms.

Alisha looked the rock over, glumly. "Let's try that bit in the middle, what do you say?"

She could feel his shrug.

"Okay. Hold on tight. Here goes nothing."

She felt his hands sliding across her belly to meet in the middle. His touch left her breathless – even under these conditions. Alisha reached out and placed her hand on the Ghama Traya and closed her eyes.

High Rise Heaven

They opened their eyes to a different landscape. Their feet stood on hard pavement, and great buildings loomed on every side. There were humans rushing about in small groups, and very few had stopped long enough to take notice of them.

"These are big houses for human peoples, yes?"

Alisha remained silent, trying to get her bearings.

"What is so big to live in these great houses?"

"Well..." She surveyed the area. They were standing in the middle of a traffic circle that had been built to accommodate the Ghama Traya either for decorative or practical reasons; it was too early to tell. "Maryland has some places that look like this. We call them 'cities,' but I do not recognize this one." She put Ahqui down. "The big houses are called 'buildings,' and they are made up of many human-sized rooms stacked on top of each other all the way to the sky. Humans live and work in these." She thought a minute. "In this way, they are like bees in a hive."

That concept, Rhamas understood. Alisha saw the smallest nod, even though his neck was craned backwards to take in the skyline.

"Does it not stink inside with so many humans living on top of each other?"

Alisha sighed. She didn't know how to answer that question.

Somewhere, a traffic light changed and a long line of cars, trucks and vans circled them in the only show that could possibly out-do that of the skyscrapers. Alisha heard Rhamas draw in his breath as Ahqui climbed her like a tree.

"Wait for the cars to stop coming and follow me." She commanded.

"Where are we going?" Rhamas asked, in awe.

"Alisha slipped into the comparative darkness of an alley and navigated piles of garbage and debris until she was certain the group was well out of sight.

She caught Ahqui's full attention, and warned him to be "sneaky-sneaky" and not wander away, then allowed him to slide down her body to the filthy concrete at her feet.

"We need a wardrobe update." She wiped a sweaty chunk of hair away from her face. "You have to be roasting inside those clothes." She argued. "Come. You must get naked and cool yourself while we figure out what you will wear."

Alisha found a spigot poking out of one of the buildings and turned it on, full. Rhamas stripped naked and did as she asked, taking every opportunity to splash great spouts of water onto Ahqui's head and body.

"This is better." He admitted, looking positively edible with water droplets sliding down his body like melted diamonds.

Rhamas turned his head just in time to find Alisha leaning over his finely-made leather pants with his hunting knife.

"What do you do!" He exclaimed, but not before Alisha had separated long sections of the legs from the main garment.

"It is too hot for these. You will be happy I did this thing." She smiled, mischievously.

Before she was done, his tunic was a sleeveless vest to his hips, and his pants had been chopped off at 'Bermuda' length. His boots had been reduced to 'booties' and, this last eventuality almost brought tears to his eyes.

"My boots!" Rhamas exclaimed. "That is ugly! What good are they in this looking?"

"Put these on, husband." She teased. "I promise to make you new ones before another winter comes."

Rhamas accepted the items, doubtfully and proceeded to dress.

Alisha examined the end result with as much optimism as she could muster. He still gave off that 'caveman' vibe, but at least he would be cooler and more comfortable.

Alisha couldn't help thinking about how lucky she was to have such a gorgeous hunk of a man to call her own. The muscles of his arms were now on full display, and the new short pants exposed his taut calves and thighs.

Rhamas read her thoughts and grinned like the devil himself.

"Yes." She admitted. "You are a very fine-looking man, Rhamas of the Jurrah tribe. My mouth waters for you, as always."

Ahqui had taken to placing himself immediately under the stream of water so that it sprayed out wildly from his head in all directions.

Alisha dug her ragged tee-shirt and jeans out of the pack and slid them on, finishing off the look with her tried-and-true rubber flip-flops.

Clean now, the group gathered to look at one another.

"Do we leave this place now, and try again?" Rhamas

asked.

"I know that was the plan, but I think these humans have things that would be helpful to us. Clothes. Shoes. Shampoo."

Alisha had spoken often of this 'shampoo,' so Rhamas knew it was something of great value to her.

"I would like to have some of these things." She said, simply, while thinking: *So that my brother won't fall onto the ground in fits of laughter when he gets a load of us while at the same time composing humorous monologues to share over holiday meals for the rest of my natural life.*

"How will you get these things without shells and hides for trade?"

Alisha wanted to be annoyed by that question, but thought the better of it. He had a point. Sort of.

"We will have to find out what they want and get some." She answered. "There are ways."

At this point, clothes foraged out of donation bins would be a big step up, wouldn't they? Alisha wondered if such a thing existed in a reality that seemed so outwardly impersonal.

"Once we have re-stocked our supplies, we will try again." She realized that the comment had sounded a lot like an order. "If that is agreeable to my handsome and very wise husband?" She was careful to add with a rueful smile.

Rhamas grinned at her concession to his pride and nodded. "I would try this Herbal Essence for full hair that you speak of."

Dynamite

Pete Larson surveyed the damage to his bull dozer. "That just beats the hell out of me." He said, under his breath. "Back-hoe couldn't dig it out?" He asked Dwayne and Scott – trusted members of his construction and demolition crew.

"Nawp. Wouldn't budge. Thing's grown clear down to the center of the earth, ya' ask me." Scott removed his hard hat and wiped a gnarled hand over his bald head.

"Gotta' dynamite it." Dwayne spat. "Ain't gonna move no other way."

The three men stood around the obstinate red rock and scratched their itchy bits. Dwayne hawked another wad of tobacco politely out of range.

"Well." Pete agreed, reluctantly. "If you've got to, you've got to. Wyndham wants it outta' here yesterday."

Everybody nodded and kicked at the dirt or brushed off their shoulders in a manly way.

"You guys get to it. I'm going to get myself some

breakfast, and I want that thing to be history before I get back."

"You got it, boss." Scott growled, thinking that he wouldn't mind a bit of something to eat, himself.

Pete hiked off to his truck and, as soon as he was out of earshot, Dwayne added: "Asshole."

"If it was me," Scott said. "I'd build around the damn thing."

"Yeah. Like, plant petunias around it or some such." Dwayne agreed.

"Some things aren't meant to be messed around with."

"I got that same feeling." Dwayne admitted, squinting at the offending boulder. "Can't say why, exactly."

"You got the key to the shed?" Scott asked.

"Yep. C'mon. Let's get this over with before that asswipe finishes his waffles."

"Right behind ya."

The men went about doing what they had to do, but neither one of them felt good about it. Not one bit.

Within the hour, the charges were set, the fuses were lit, and the red rock was nothing but a distant memory.

The Earthquake

Alisha wrapped Ahqui up in a bit of the white leather to disguise his tail. The humans had not so much as glanced in their direction, but it never hurt to blend in.

They stepped out of the cooler shadows and into the unbearable heat of a concrete oven not unlike New York or Chicago. Busy humans walked here and there with a purpose – eyes locked on their destinations and completely devoid of curiosity.

"Which way?" Rhamas asked, once again craning his neck to gauge the height of the buildings.

But, Alisha's eyes were on the Ghama Traya squatting in the middle of its concrete island. It was breaking apart. A great crack had appeared near the middle and was widening aggressively as she watched. It was shortly thereafter that the ground had begun to shudder ominously.

Ahqui shrieked a warning and attempted to climb onto Alisha's head.

"Rhamas!" Alisha cried.

The ground began to lurch crazily beneath their feet and humans started to pour out of the buildings like salt from a shaker.

"The Gods are angry!" Rhamas called, sweeping Alisha off her feet – Ahqui still clutching handfuls of her hair – and running with both of them through the crowds and down the main street with no clear destination in mind. "Many will die. We must leave this place!"

"Ouch!" Alisha cried, grabbing frantically to untangle the squear from her hair. "Rhamas! Put me down!"

But, the quaking continued with increasing violence, and soon great chunks of concrete and sheets of glass were tumbling from impossible heights to the streets below, only to explode like grenades when they reached the pavement.

Rhamas ran on. He dodged every obstacle – be it human or otherwise – with amazing finesse, and never slowed or allowed his loved ones to slip so much as an inch from his grasp.

At long last, Rhamas pulled to a stop in a great, wide circle that had been created to accommodate vendors and gatherings. It was here that Rhamas set Alisha down, gently, and helped to extricate the hysterical squear from her tangled mane.

Crowds began to assemble around them in small groupings of three or four. Voices rose and fell like the cries of cicadas in a forest. Some sat while others stood or leaned against benches or streetlights. Their clothing was not eccentric or alien to Alisha in any way. Some wore suits, dresses and heels, while others seemed more casual in shorts, jeans or tees. Everyone was coated in a film of white dust. It was hard to breathe.

"Thank you." Alisha whispered, pulling Rhamas down beside her. "That was quick thinking."

Ahqui seconded the motion by climbing into Rhamas's lap and curling into the crook of one of his arms like an adoring son.

"Our packs are back there." Rhamas said, pointing.

"It is not our packs that I am worried about." Alisha dropped her head onto her knees.

A silence fell between them as the reality dawned on Rhamas.

"The Ghama Traya?" He asked.

"Gone." She lifted her head.

"We are here forever, then?"

"We are here, forever, my husband."

"We will like it here?" He asked through a throat choked with dust.

"We will have to." She answered. Alisha leaned her head against his shoulder and the three of them huddled among strangers made of chalk and surrounded by clouds of finite debris.

Nearby, Alisha heard someone say, "That's another station down. It'll be crap getting home for Christmas this year."

She lifted her head. "That was English!" She whispered urgently. "Rhamas! That couple speaks Maryland!"

Made in the USA
Monee, IL
19 October 2023